DATE DUE

MAY 1 1 2004	
JUL 2 7 2005	
WITHDRAWN	

The Moonlighters

The Moonlighters

RAY HOGAN

Sagebrush
Large Print Westerns

Library of Congress Cataloging in Publication Data

Hogan, Ray
    The moonlighters / Ray Hogan
        p. cm.
    ISBN 1-57490-003-X
    1. Large type books.   I. Title.
813' .52—dc20

Cataloguing in Publication Data is available from
the British Library and the National Library of Australia.

Sagebrush Large Print Westerns are published in the
United States and Canada by Thomas T. Beeler, Publisher,
P.O. Box 659, Hampton Falls, New Hampshire 03844-0659.
ISBN 1-57490-003-X

Published in the United Kingdom, Eire, and the Republic of
South Africa by Isis Publishing Ltd, 7 Centremead, Osney
Mead, Oxford OX2 0ES England. ISBN 1-85695-299-1

Published in Australia and New Zealand by Australian Large
Print Audio & Video Pty Ltd, 15 Mohr Street, Tullamarine,
Victoria, 3043, Australia. ISBN 1-86340-577-1

Manufactured in the United States of America

CHAPTER ONE

Whiterock...

Standing in the shadows at the corner of the Border Queen Saloon, Frank Sanderson let his glance run down the dusty street. A few persons, taking their ease in the evening coolness, strolled the board sidewalks. Most of the stores had closed, and only a scattering of windows glowed from inner lamps. The general store was still open; so also were the bakery, the saddle-and-gun shop, and, of course, the saloons and livery stables.

"Just like a hundred other towns," he muttered. "Been better if we'd kept going until we hit Tucson."

"Tucson ain't got a fat bank just waiting to be plucked," Harvey Neff said, pulling himself away from the wall. A handsome, dark man, he had spent most of his life in the Army, and it still showed in the way he held himself upright, almost stiff. "Enough gold eagles in that cracker box—just waiting for us—to keep us till doomsday."

Sanderson shook his head. "Count me out."

Immediately Neff turned. "Why? You ain't a lawman no more—and you're flat busted, just like Virg and me. You got something against being rich?"

1

"Not against being rich—against the way you're wanting to get it."

Neff snorted. "What's the difference? Man's smart to look out for himself—take things as they come. Hell, you'll make more'n five minutes in this than you could in fifteen years at that town-marshal job you got kicked out of. Ain't that so?"

Sanderson stirred, slightly angered. Kansas Bend was in the past—Kansas Bend with its hard-nosed people and two-bit tin-star job. He didn't like to think about it. They'd been wrong—and maybe he'd been wrong. Let it go at that. But he reckoned an ex-lawman couldn't shuck his convictions as easily as a cashiered Army officer. He was down to his last three dollars—sure. And the Bank of Whiterock looked like an easy touch. But the thought of robbery…

"What do you say, Virg?" Neff's voice was soft in the dark.

Frank watched the slight figure of Virgil Peck turn slowly. Virgil was a shotgun guard for a stage line—or had been until a road agent had put three bullets into his body and crippled him up a bit. Since then he hired out now and then as a fast gun. Like Sanderson and Neff, he was footloose and down on his luck.

"Well, robbing banks ain't my specialty," he drawled, "but I'm game as the next man. Leave it up to Frank."

Harvey Neff swore. "Goddammit—this ain't

2

getting us nowhere. Going around in circles. Be nothing to it, busting into that building and helping ourselves to all the gold eagles we can tote off."

Sanderson shrugged. "You're like all the rest of them," he said. "Jails are full of jaspers who thought something like this would be easy. Trouble with that kind of thinking is, you never figure on the other side having any sense."

"You're talking like a lawman again."

"Maybe. But there's a few things I know about a deal like this that you don't. I've been on the other end of it...

Neff started a reply, then cut it off as a man and a woman moved by, both laughing at something that had been said. Music from the Border Queen was trickling into the street, and somewhere among the scatter of houses behind them a gunshot sounded.

"You think they're not keeping a tight watch on that gold they hauled in today?" Sanderson continued. "Hell, with a payroll that size the place will be crawling with deputies."

"Had me a close look inside the bank," Neff replied, a note of doubt creeping into his tone. "Never saw anybody."

"They're there," Sanderson said. "Even if I was of a mind to make my pile that way, I'd steer clear of that place. One-way ticket to hell."

"Then—for crissake—*you* think of a way to raise some money!" Neff snapped, rough and impatient. "Had my belly full of going around

3

ragged-assed and broke!"

"Stage coming," Virg Peck commented as a rattle of chains and thud of hoofs sounded at the far end of the street.

Sanderson, lifting his gaze, watched the vehicle career around the corner and rush to a stop at the hotel a few doors below the Border Queen. A hostler came from the darkness beyond the two-story structure and halted, hands on hips, while the driver climbed down, moved to the coach door and opened it. A lone passenger emerged.

Neff emitted a low whistle. "Judas—what a woman!"

Sanderson gave her a second glance, finding something familiar in the slim, graceful figure in a dove-gray suit. She wasn't young—somewhere in her late twenties or possibly early thirties, he guessed—nor was she particularly beautiful; but there was about her a coolness, a quiet reserve that was beauty in itself. Striking—he guessed that was the word for her.

He watched her turn and look up the street, then down. Her eyes paused on him, touched Neff and Virg Peck briefly, came back. She smiled as if she too were remembering.

Harvey Neff groaned faintly. "Man could die happy—going to bed with that."

"Your bag, Missus London," the driver said, placing a suitcase on the walk beside her. "Boy, there'll carry it inside for you."

"Who you reckon she is?" Neff wondered.

Recognition had come to Frank Sanderson. "Name's Kate London. Was a blackjack dealer in an El Paso saloon."

The Army man turned to him. "You know her?"

Sanderson shrugged. "Was down there once for a couple of days. Played a few hands at her table."

Kate said several words to the hostler, who picked up her bag and, abandoning his chores with the horses, started for the lobby of the hotel. She turned toward the three men, a faint smile on her lips.

Neff swore in quiet desperation. "Seems she recollects you," Virg Peck said. "You sure all you done was some card playing, Frank?"

Sanderson didn't reply. Kate London moved up and extended her gloved hand.

"Evening, Marshal. Good to see you again."

Frank removed his hat and enclosed her fingers in his. "Good to see you, Mrs. London. But it's not Marshal any more."

She glanced questioningly at him, then looked at Neff and Peck. Sanderson introduced both men, adding, "I quit that job."

Kate's brows lifted in surprise. Then, shrugging, she said, "I suppose change comes to all of us."

"That mean you've left El Paso?"

She nodded, looking directly at him. "What are you doing nowadays?"

"Looking for a job. All three of us."

A pleased smile parted her lips. "That's fortunate for me! I intend to hire several men to do a job. Had figured to look around for a week or two until I found just the ones I wanted. Running into you makes that unnecessary."

"What kind of a job?" Sanderson asked.

She hesitated momentarily, then said, "I suppose you could call it an escort party."

"Escorting you, that it?"

"That's it. But it's all too involved to discuss here in the street. Why don't you—all of you—come to the hotel in about an hour? I'll tell you about it there."

Frank Sanderson made no answer. Kate sensed the reason for his reluctance.

"It'll be lawful work—I'll not be asking you to do anything wrong. And I'm willing to pay you each a thousand dollars for doing it."

A thousand dollars—each! Sanderson felt surprise roll through him. Kate London apparently had something big going. He nodded.

"We'll be there," he said. "One hour."

CHAPTER TWO

One hour later by the clock Sanderson, flanked by Neff and Virgil Peck, rapped on the door to Kate London's room.

She opened the scarred panel immediately and stepped back. "Come in, gentlemen."

6

The gray traveling suit had been exchanged for a simple, lightweight dress of blue that brought out the color of her eyes, and her dark hair, piled high on her head, glowed from the lamplight. She was, Sanderson had to admit, a fine-looking woman, if a bit cold and remote. She pointed to chairs placed near the open window.

"Sit there, please," she said, a trace of southern accent rounding the edges of her words. "You'll find it a bit more comfortable."

The men settled themselves. Kate found a place on the edge of the bed. She sat for a few minutes studying her clasped hands, listening to the sounds in the street below. Finally she glanced up.

"I know you're wondering about the job I mentioned. I'll come right to the point—but first, there's just one thing."

Sanderson reached for his tobacco and papers and began to roll himself a cigarette.

"I want your promise that nothing you hear will be repeated outside this room. It's important."

Frank nodded, passing the muslin sack to Peck.

"You've got it."

"And if you decide you don't want the job— you'll forget everything I've told you."

Sanderson bobbed his head again. Harvey Neff, smiling, said, "You can depend on it, ma'am. And a gentleman always keeps his

7

promise to a beautiful woman."

Kate smiled, but her smile had no depth. She knew Neff's type and had long ago schooled herself to tolerate it.

"I don't think any of you knew my husband—or rather, my second husband. His name was Dan London. He was a prospector. We had been married about eleven years, although I saw very little of him during that time. Not too long ago, he rode into El Paso to tell me that he had finally struck it rich." She paused, staring at the floor. "He was almost dead. He'd been shot twice."

"Shot?" Neff repeated. "By who?"

Kate shook her head. "I don't know. He died that same night." Again she hesitated. "Poor Dan. He might be alive today if he had stopped somewhere, had his wounds attended to. But he was so anxious to reach me—tell me about this great fortune he had found—"

Sanderson was beginning to understand. "This job you're talking about: you want us to go after the gold—that it?"

Kate London said, "That's it."

"Where is it?"

"In the Peloncillo Mountains."

"Peloncillos?" Peck echoed, surprised. "Never heard of gold in that country."

"It's there," she said. "I guarantee that."

"Five days' hard riding from here," Peck commented. "Sure was anxious to tell you about it—if the shooting took place in the Peloncillos."

"So much it cost him his life," she said simply.

Dan London must have thought a lot of his wife, Sanderson realized. He glanced at Kate and for a few moments studied the smooth, soft contours of her face. He guessed he could understand the man. But the cynical streak that possessed him where gold mines filled with fabulous treasures were concerned pushed aside that thought.

"Not much for wild-goose chasing."

"Be nothing like that. We'll have no trouble finding the gold."

Sanderson considered her words. The Peloncillo range lay near the corner formed by the junction of New Mexico, Arizona and Mexico. It was Apache Indian country, frequented also by outlaws from both sides of the border. Smugglers coming up from Mexico City and other points used it on their treks to Tucson, preferring it to the more southerly trail through Skeleton Canyon, in the Guadalupe chain.

"No place for a woman," he said. "Tough even for a man to get around."

"I'll be all right."

"Is this a mine, or is the gold out—buried somewheres?" Neff asked.

Kate toyed with the folds of her skirt. "There's no mine. The gold's in sacks. Dan hid it."

"How much?" The Army man's eyes had

9

taken on a brighter light as his interest mounted.

"A great deal. That's why I can offer each of you a thousand dollars. Your job will simply be to take me in, so I can get the treasure, and bring me out. I'm hiring you and your guns—and you stick with me no matter what happens; I've got to have your word on that."

Sanderson frowned. "You expecting trouble?"

"No, but I don't fancy the thought of getting deep in those mountains and then having you change your minds and pull out."

"No chance of that," Frank said, faintly angered. He still didn't like the idea of her going. "Best if you just give us a map, wait here. Woman always draws trouble that otherwise might pass us by."

"I must go," she said firmly. "It's part of the deal—the job. You'd never find the gold without me, anyway."

There's also a little matter of trust, Sanderson thought, reading her mind. She was afraid that once they had the treasure in their possession, they might keep on going with it. It was a natural suspicion. After all, they were more or less strangers.

"I'll be no problem," she continued. "Far as you're concerned, I'll be just another man in the party."

Harvey Neff canted his head, grinning appreciatively. "Doubt if anybody'd look at it that way." He turned to Sanderson. "She'll be fine.

10

I'll make it my job to look after her."

"No need for that," Kate cut in quietly, her tone cool.

Attempting to dissuade her was hopeless, Frank saw. But there would be trouble regardless of what she thought, if only from Harvey Neff. The Army man would have to be straightened out before the trip ever began.

"When do you want to pull out?"

Relief crossed Kate London's face. "As soon as possible."

"What about gear? We'll be needing pack mules, a horse for you, grub..."

"If you'll help, we can make all those arrangements in the morning. Perhaps we could leave tomorrow afternoon."

"Better figure the next day—sunrise. Don't want to get in a rush, forget something."

Kate got to her feet, bringing the men upright. She extended her hand to Sanderson, enclosing his with a firm clasp.

"Then it's agreed. I have your word and promise."

Frank nodded, and she solemnly went through a like ritual with Virg Peck and Harvey Neff while he thought, *What a crew! A crippled gunman, a busted Army officer, a washed-up lawman, and a card-sharp widow, all hooked together on a treasure hunt. A fine bunch of moonlighters!*

"We'll meet downstairs for breakfast," he heard her say. "Six o'clock."

11

"Six o'clock," he repeated, and he opened the door.

There was a quick thumping sound in the hallway. Sanderson stepped out fast and glanced in both directions. There was no one in sight, and all was quiet. He shook his head, guessing it had been his imagination—but he could have sworn—

"I'm looking forward to a most enjoyable trip," Harvey Neff said in his most careful voice. "And I shall do my best to see that you're comfortable."

"I expect no comfort," Kate London replied coolly. "It is purely a matter of business. I intend to keep it that way. Good night, gentlemen."

Sanderson touched the brim of his hat. The others paid their courtesies and all went down into the lobby and out onto the porch. Frank wheeled on Neff. "Let's get something straight, Harvey: You got any ideas about Kate London—forget them until we're back!"

The Army man bristled. "What the hell's that mean? You making her your private property?"

"Not by a damn sight—but we'll have plenty of problems without you adding to them."

Neff shrugged. "She's of age—and a widow to boot. I figure things'll be up to her. Let *her* decide."

"She won't need to decide anything if you're not pushing her. I'm telling you now: Forget it or back off. This deal's got a bad smell to me anyway. Got a hunch we're heading into more than we're bargaining for."

"Something you ain't spoke up about?" Peck asked, rubbing at his jaw.

"Just a feeling." Sanderson started to mention the probability that someone had been outside Kate London's door listening, then decided to let it go; he had nothing solid upon which to base the belief. "Going to have to be on our toes all the time—every one of us."

"Way I look at it," Peck said, and he turned to face Neff squarely. "Get your mind made up, Harvey. If you're aiming on a lot of foolishness, say so now, so's we can rustle up another man. Reckon it won't be hard to do."

"Hell with that!" Neff shot back angrily. "That thousand looks as big to me as it does to you. I'm coming along. And don't do no fretting over me and the lady; that'll take care of itself."

Abruptly he wheeled about and headed for the Border Queen. Sanderson and Peck watched him until he pushed through the bat-wing doors and was lost to sight. The little gunman sighed.

"I'm hoping that thousand *does* mean something to him—enough to keep him straight, anyway."

"Going to be a hard choice for him to make," Frank said, moving off into the street. "Let's get some sleep."

13

CHAPTER THREE

Kate London stood at her window and looked down onto the street. She could hear the low mutter of the three men's voices coming from somewhere below, but there was no making out their words. A few moments later Neff, who unquestionably considered himself the answer to every maiden's dream, stepped into view and hurried toward the Border Queen Saloon. Then Sanderson and Peck came into her line of vision and strode off into the night.

She turned back into the room, her mind now at ease. It had gone much more easily than she had expected—but she should have guessed that it would.

Gold was the magic key where men were concerned and offering each a thousand dollars had turned the trick. Let the poets rave all they wanted about faith, hope, charity, and the delights of being nonmaterialistic—it was hard cash that spoke the language men understood; it was in gold that they found the beginning and the end.

It was the end for Dan London, she thought, pausing in the center of the stuffy room, just as it had been for Dandy Beaumont, her first husband. And there was no denying, money had been a prominent, motivating factor in the years of her own life.

Daughter of a Louisiana planter, Kate had

met Dandy, a riverboat gambler with swash-buckling ways, at the tender age of fifteen. She was a mother at sixteen, a widow before seventeen. Disowned by an outraged family, she soon drifted west with a tide of other hopeful souls, searching, as were they, for a new life.

During that hectic period she did all things possible to keep her infant daughter, Marguerite, and herself alive, but quickly discovered her greatest talent lay in the skill of her slender fingers and their ability to manipulate cards at the gambling tables. Thus she became a dealer. It was the one thing for which she could be grateful to Dandy Beaumont; he had taught her well.

Eventually she halted in the border settlement of El Paso, determined to make there a permanent home for Marguerite and herself. But El Paso and its tough Mexican counterpart across the Rio Grande were rugged, violent towns and no proper atmosphere for the gentle upbringing of a child. Kate found it a full-time chore just to look after herself.

By accident she heard of a convent operated by a church order known as the Sisters of Sorrow. It was in San Antonio, quite a distance away. She debated for a time the wisdom of placing Marguerite in the care of the nuns, then finally decided it was the only thing to do.

Kate London had not seen her daughter since. Often she had intended to go there and pay Marguerite a visit, but somehow it never came to pass. It was a dusty, disagreeable ride that consumed several days going and coming—and a convenient time for the arduous journey never presented itself.

She was able to send a little money periodically for the child's upkeep, always with a letter advising the nuns of her intention to reclaim her daughter; but somehow fate and the turn of the cards consistently managed to thwart her best designs.

For one thing, Dan London, whom she married not long after placing Marguerite in the convent, was a man who wanted no children; and while he was aware of the girl's existence and never openly expressed opposition to Kate's hope of being reunited with her daughter, he made it amply clear in many ways that he was opposed to the idea.

It would have been impractical, anyway. Dan was a good man but one entirely beyond his depth in the frontier world into which he had stumbled. He never quite belonged to or became, a part of it—and he had absolutely no talent for making a living.

Thus Kate was forced to retain her job at the card tables, supporting herself as best she could while London floundered aimlessly from one hare-brained scheme to another. During the period of their marriage he undertook scores of projects, all sure-fire roads to riches, and all failed.

But at the price of his life, Dan London had

16

finally come through. The gold was there, just waiting for her, he had declared with his fading breath. Three chests...heavy with gold coin...Mexican *reales*. It would amount to fifty thousand American dollars, maybe more. All Kate need do was go where he had hidden it—and get what was hers.

And get it she would—no matter what the cost. She had earned it—was entitled to it. And Frank Sanderson and Virgil Peck and Harvey Neff would make it all possible. Then the world would be hers and Marguerite's.

Once she had the gold and was back in civilization, that would be her first move: She would hurry to the convent at San Antonio and get her daughter. Marguerite would be almost seventeen now. A young lady—likely a most beautiful one. The girl had favored them both, but mostly she had resembled Dandy, with his black, curly hair and laughing eyes.

Her beauty would not be wasted. She would never know the pillar-to-post existence her mother had been compelled to endure. They would go east, back to the big cities...New York...perhaps Philadelphia. There she would have everything a rich young girl should have. She would meet and marry a man of consequence. There would be no Dandy Beaumonts to sweep her off her feet, no Dan Londons to support. Marguerite would know the good life.

Oh—it was wonderful to know that things were finally going to work out right, that things

17

would be different not only for her daughter but for herself.

Sighing, Kate London sat down at the battered washstand and pushed the bowl and pitcher aside. Taking a pencil and a sheet of paper, she put her mind to making a list of the supplies they would need for the trip into the Peloncillos and back. Food for four persons—for two weeks. Pots, pans, blankets. She'd leave the pack mules and the horse for her use up to Sanderson. Canteens—she had almost forgotten them. Best have Sanderson go over the list with her, see if there were other necessary items she had overlooked.

When that was done, she arose and moved to the dresser. Shifting the lamp to a better position, she examined her reflection critically. A sort of contentment was flowing through her, along with a deep satisfaction. It was hard to believe the fortune of which she had always dreamed was almost within her grasp. Another week—one week—and all that gold would be in her possession!

It had been fortunate she had recognized Frank Sanderson there on the street. Otherwise she could have wasted days finding a suitable man to head up the party for her. The one-time lawman was the perfect choice: tough, unafraid, respected by his companions—and smart. She couldn't expect to keep him in the dark for long—but maybe her luck would hold until they reached the Peloncillos and located the treasure.

18

Once they were on the way, things would shape up all right. Even if Sanderson grew suspicious, he wouldn't walk out on her. She had forced him to give his word, and he was one of those who'd never go back on a promise. With him a deal was a deal—and equally important, he was honest. Whatever it was that had caused him to turn his back on the law could not have been any fault of his; she had not spent all those years behind the gambling tables without learning how to judge the qualities of men.

Neff was something else. He was the unpredictable type, the kind who would try anything if there were sufficient reason. Vain, equally honest or dishonest depending upon the circumstances, he would bear watching. She wondered why he was no longer in the Army. The odds were ten to one there had been a woman involved in his trouble.

And Virgil Peck. She knew nothing about him other than that he looked like a killer. He made her remember some of the flat-eyed men who had drifted into El Paso on their way to Mexico, where they would be safe from the law. They had always filled her with a slight chill. She was glad Peck would be with them on the trip to the Peloncillos. He would be good to have along in event of trouble.

And there could be trouble. Dan London, in a feverish delirium for most of the long ride from where he had cached the gold, had undoubtedly raved about the treasure he had discovered.

There would be many who had heard. Some would have dismissed it as the rantings of a man out of his mind, but there could have been those who did not, who listened.

Did Dan reveal the exact location of the hidden gold?

She had voiced that fear to him during the final, lucid hours before death claimed him. He assured her there was no need for worry; he had never divulged the hiding place of the chests, only spoken of their existence. She hoped and prayed that such was true.

Kate wondered then if she should have mentioned that possibility to Frank Sanderson, then decided it was as well she had not; it might have influenced his decision to accept her offer. Not that he would be afraid; she doubted that Frank Sanderson had known fear in his entire life; but he could have considered the possibilities and decided that probably the gold was gone, that the trip would be for nothing.

She began to undress and prepare herself for bed.

She'd sleep on the matter. In the morning, if she felt he should know, she would tell him. That would be soon enough.

From the shadows gathered along the side of Damon's Barber Shop, Billy Farr watched as Kate London's window went dark.

Earlier he had seen the three men who had been in her room come from the hotel, pause for a short time on the porch, and then separate. All

20

were strangers to him.

Kate had made some sort of deal with them—exactly what he was unsure, but that it had to do with the gold Dan London had cached he was certain. Listening at her door, he had overheard that much.

That was fine, he thought, removing his hat and brushing nervously at his hair. He had young, boyish features and a quick, anxious way about him. It meant Kate was starting the last leg of the journey, that she was now heading for the spot where her husband had buried the treasure he had raved about.

Billy Farr grinned wolfishly into the night. Kate London didn't know it, but he'd be along too. He'd followed her all the way from El Paso, and her signing on three hard cases to side her wasn't going to turn him back now. Billy Farr was cutting himself in on that gold—and nothing was going to stop him!

CHAPTER FOUR

They left Whiterock well before dawn with sunrise only a gray hint in the east. Kate London was very secretive about it all, making it plain she had as soon no one in the settlement became aware of their departure. She and Sanderson were in the lead, followed by Virgil Peck and Harvey Neff. Behind them came the pack mules—tough, wiry little beasts, all heavily loaded.

If there was anyone abroad who saw them leave, Frank missed him. Some of Kate's caution had rubbed off on him, and he gave the dusty street, with its square-topped buildings etched blackly against the sky, a thorough search when they reached its end. There had been no sign of witnesses.

As they rode in silence along the rutted road, Sanderson took more lengthy note of Kate London. She had exchanged her stylish dress for serviceable denim and coarse shirtwaist. Durable knee boots sheathed her feet and legs, and she had gathered her wealth of dark hair under a wide-brimmed hat.

She sat the sorrel he had picked for her with ease and confidence—a fact that pleased him considerably. Earlier, he had entertained misgivings as to her familiarity with horses. It would be bad enough to have a woman on such a tiring, risky venture, but to have been saddled with a female greenhorn—his sigh was deep and grateful that he had been spared that.

A short time later, just after they had veered from the road and taken to open country, the sun began to probe the irregular rim to the east, shooting up long fingers of gray into the dark curve of the sky. A soft wind began to stir, and the night's chill became more pronounced, as though reluctant to yield to the approaching day.

If Kate noticed the cold, she gave no indication. Her eyes were straight ahead, fixed on the silver-tinged land that rose and fell in deceptively smooth undulations until it faded into infinity. Grotesque cholla, twisted junipers, and gaunt mesquite trees silhouetted against the ghostly background, and in the half-light a vivid patch of deep-red flowers glowed on a nearby slope.

"The desert is a beautiful place—a world of its own," she murmured, more to herself than to Sanderson.

He grunted. "Maybe. By noon, the devil could use it for hell."

"I know. But still it's beautiful."

"Only the top you're looking at."

She turned to him. "You sound as if you hate it."

He shrugged. "Not hate. Respect. I know the desert. Man can die out there without half trying. It's like a pool of quicksand—smooth, quiet, but plenty treacherous."

"No different from life itself," she said, and she looked away.

They continued in silence. Behind them the searching tentacles above the rim had changed from gray to orange and now were beginning to fuse into a vast fan of yellow as the sun broke over the horizon. The wind died, and the first thin threads of warmth made themselves felt.

The world around them began to take form and substance as its soft edges vanished. The

23

cholla, the tortured junipers, and other desert growth now appeared baked, dull gray, and scarcely alive. Harsh reds and yellows, intermixed with faded browns and tans, blurred the landscape, and the sandy floor beneath them became a glittering carpet that pained the eyes.

By ten o'clock the heat was intense and brutal, with the worst yet to come. Sanderson gauged the horses critically. They were still in good shape, but it would be wise to spare them. The party dipped into a steep-walled, greasewood-choked arroyo, disturbing a long-eared jackrabbit that raced off into the brush in soaring leaps.

"Fifteen-minute rest," Sanderson called over his shoulder as he halted.

All dismounted, Neff cranky and gaunt. He moved up to where Kate and Sanderson stood in the thin shade of the brush. Mopping his face, he glanced about irritably.

"God—what a country. You sure you know where you're going?"

Frank answered, "I know."

Kate removed her hat and began to fan herself. High above them a half a dozen vultures, instantly attracted by their stopping, began to circle slowly. There was a slight commotion near the mules as a rattlesnake slithered into view, paused, then serpentined its way back into hiding as Peck shied a rock at it.

The one-time Army officer cocked his head to stare at the birds soaring above them. "You sure better know what you're doing. Otherwise we're buzzard bait."

"We'll make it," Sanderson said. "Let's go."

Neff muttered something and turned away. Sanderson helped Kate into her saddle, then climbed onto his own horse. He glanced over his shoulder at the rest of the party. All were ready. He touched the chestnut with his spurs and they moved on.

In single file they crossed the floor of the arroyo and clambered up the opposite side. Again on the burning level of the shimmering mesa, Frank looked ahead. Still a long way to go, but by nightfall...

"Sanderson—"

Virg Peck's laconic voice brought him around.

"Yeh?"

"We got company."

CHAPTER FIVE

Frank Sanderson saw Kate's features tighten, her lips compress into a straight line. He frowned and turned to squint into the distance behind them. Four riders hung against a background of yellow dust and spinning heat waves.

"Think they're dogging us?" Peck asked.

The lawman shrugging, said, "I'm wondering."

Coincidence was possible, of course, but it didn't seem likely. The horsemen were far off the main trail; pilgrims headed west crossed more to the south, along the border, or stuck to the well-traveled route that skirted the northern end of the Peloncillos. Only someone with a specific reason—such as theirs—would aim directly for the heart of the rugged range. Stirred by suspicion, Sanderson turned to Kate.

"This why you wanted to get out of town early without being seen?"

Kate shook her head. "That was just a precaution," she said coolly.

"You think those four men are following us?"

"I don't know any more about them than you do."

Sweat was seeping from every pore in Sanderson's body, and that irritation heightened his anger. "Happens I think you do! Who are they?"

Again she moved her head. "I've no idea—regardless of what you think."

He shifted on the saddle, eyes never leaving her face. "As I understood this deal, nobody else knew where your husband buried that gold."

"No one did—no one that I'm aware of." Kate paused, then went on. "There's a chance somebody could have listened to him while he was out of his head with fever. He was that way, I suspect, all the way to El Paso."

Dead silence followed Kate's words. A whip-tailed lizard sprawled under a flat rock, tongue

26

out, watched them with beady eyes. One of the mules stamped and switched his tail at a cloud of aggravating gnats hovering around his hindquarters.

"Godalmighty!" Peck groaned finally. "Every jack-leg drifter and owl-hoot between the Arkansas River and the border's probably on our trail!"

Sanderson studied the distant quartet. "Best thing we can do is figure on it."

"We are figuring on it," Kate London said quietly. "That's why you're all here. I considered the possibility of others trying to find the gold, take it from me. You're my protection. A thousand dollars each and your word guarantees that."

Neff laughed. Peck looked to Sanderson. "What's our next move?"

Frank settled himself squarely on his saddle and fixed his gaze on the country ahead. "Start hiding our trail, keep out of sight best we can."

"Reckon them four ain't the only ones," Peck said then. "Two more dust spirals—to the south."

Sanderson wheeled around and stared at the dust boils. Both were smaller than the one created by the party of four. Single riders, possibly.

"Moving this way," Neff said. "Probably got the same idea as the others."

It would be smart to assume as much, Sanderson thought. "We're caught in the middle. Got to figure, on sidetracking them."

27

"Could drop back a piece, set us up an ambush," Virg Peck suggested, direct and to the point in his methods.

Frank shook his head. "Whoever that is south of us don't know where we are yet. Gunshots would give us away."

"Then what'll we do?" Neff demanded. "Setting here ain't helping none."

Sanderson, ignoring him, pointed to a low roll of ground some distance ahead of them. "That bunch back of us have seen us. Can't afford to let them think we know they're on our trail. Likely there's another arroyo on the yonder side of that rise. We'll start our dodging there."

"Still be tracks they can follow," Neff pointed out.

"What I'm planning on," the lawman said, and touching Kate with his glance, he put the chestnut into motion.

They continued, neither slackening nor increasing their pace. They topped the rise. Below them a wide, sandy-floored gash in the desert angled off, taking a more-or-less east-to-west course. Sanderson led the party down the abrupt slope and swung right. Immediately Neff challenged him.

"What the hell you doing—doubling back?"

"Not yet," Sanderson replied patiently. "You called it back there; they'll see our tracks."

"Then just how in—"

"Button your lip and wait," Virg Peck cut in,

suddenly fed up with Neff's interference. "Expect Frank knows what he's up to."

The Army man fell silent for a long moment. Then, "He sure better. If he doesn't, we're done for."

Sanderson, slightly out in front of the others, rode on, eyes probing the country ahead. It was near midday, and the sun's rays beat down like white-hot lances, spearing their flesh, draining every drop of moisture from their bodies. They should halt, he knew, but now suddenly, thanks to Kate London's neglect in telling all, time had become important and a precious commodity that must not be wasted.

He continued to search the glistening floor of the channel up which they wound their way. Then he abruptly settled back, satisfaction filling his smarting eyes. A second arroyo slanted off from the main wash, angling to the west and the smudge of hills now coming into focus. It was what he had hoped for. When they reached the division, he drew to a halt.

"Keep going," he said, motioning to Kate and Harvey Neff. "I'll catch up."

Then he dropped back to Peck, coming up with the mules. Pointing down the branch draw, he said, "Take them through there. And keep going. We'll join you later."

Peck nodded, turned his horse into the arroyo, and led the pack animals into its narrow confines. Frank, freeing his brush jacket from the cantle, leaned far over and began to wipe

29

out the hoofprints that would have indicated where the little gunman had turned off. That done, he hurried to overtake Kate and Harvey Neff, now a long hundred yards farther on.

Kate London glanced at him questioningly. He only nodded, still simmering slightly.

"What's going on?" Neff wanted to know.

"Keep riding," Sanderson replied, moving again into the lead. "We're making those tracks you mentioned."

"Have to spell these horses pretty soon," the Army man warned. "Sun's taking the starch out of them."

"They'll last until we catch up with Virg."

The horses were not alone in their need for rest. Kate, Frank saw, was near exhaustion. She was slumped on the saddle, easing herself by pressing down with both hands on the horn. Her face was streaked with dust, and several strands of hair had escaped her hat and now hung untidily about her neck.

She rode with her eyes closed, leaving it up to the sorrel.

Remorse stirred him. He had been a little sharp with her—but most of this could have been avoided if he had known all the facts ahead of time. For Neff's suffering he had no compassion. If the Army officer had forgone his taste for whiskey the previous night and gotten some rest instead of spending his time in the Border Queen, he would now be in much better condition. For himself, he'd manage. He was good for a few more hours.

They followed the burning floor of the wash for a full mile. Then, when the surface became rock-studded and hard-packed, Sanderson led them out of the gash and into the brush that studded its left bank. Halting there, he turned his attention to the opposite direction. They were still below the rise; the four riders could not be seen.

"Let's catch up with Virg," he said, and he struck off through the creosote bush and other rank growth. "Watch close. Don't get on any hills."

Sanderson's strategy was now plain to all: The four riders, if they were actually trailing them, would drop into the main arroyo and continue to follow the hoofprints pressed deep into the loose sand. Since Frank had obliterated the tracks where Peck and the mules had turned off, they would miss the turn-off and follow the plainly visible tracks of the others.

When they reached the rocks they would lose the trail, but since Sanderson and his party had been bearing due north, they would undoubtedly push on. With luck, it would be hours before they discovered their error; and by then miles would separate them and darkness would have closed in.

An hour later they overtook Peck and dropped into the wash along which he was leading the mules. The rise still protected them, and Sanderson was certain they had not been observed.

"We stopping here?" Neff called.

Frank pointed ahead. "Not yet. Better get as far from that arroyo as we can."

Harvey Neff swore, but stayed in the saddle.

As minutes dragged by, the heat seemed to grow in fury, but eventually they reached an area where the ravine flattened and spilled down into a shallow bowl in the cup of three hills. Sanderson called a halt and, dismounting, made his way to the crest of the highest knoll. Flat on his belly, he looked toward the upper end of the arroyo. Relief flowed through him. The men had gained the rocks and were moving on. They had fallen for the ruse.

He returned to the hollow, some of the hard tension gone from him. "We're rid of them— leastwise for a spell," he said. "Now we start thinking about the others."

Kate only nodded soberly, but he could see a break in the tautness that had gripped her. Neff, sprawled in the shade thrown by the horses, looked up.

"We camping here?"

Sanderson shook his head and pointed toward a line of ragged hills rising blue-gray to the west. "That's where we'll bed down."

"Not me," Neff said promptly. "Right here's good enough. I'm staying put."

The lawman shrugged and said, "Suit yourself."

But later, after they had resumed the trail, he

32

glanced back. The Army man, he saw, had mounted his dust-caked horse and was bringing up the rear.

CHAPTER SIX

They reached the cluster of hills, a detached spur off the Peloncillo range, well after sundown. Sweaty, morose, and uncaring after the day's savage treatment, they rode silently into the clearing of a deep hollow.

Dismounting, they immediately began to strip the animals of their gear, going about the chore wearily and mechanically. There was little grass in the rock-studded cup, and Sanderson brought out nose bags and dipped into the sacks of grain the stableman had provided. There was no spring; they were compelled to fall back on their canteens to satisfy the thirst of the horses and mules, and since they had no other sizable containers, they made use of their hats.

The last to finish his task, Sanderson walked heavily into the clearing to find Neff gathering sticks in its center preparatory to building a fire.

"Forget it," the lawman said gruffly, kicking the pile of wood aside.

Kate rummaging about in the supplies, paused. Peck, sitting on the still-warm ground, head resting on forearms folded across his knees, raised his head slowly.

33

Half upright, Harvey Neff stared at Sanderson. His eyes were bloodshot, and dust rimmed his mouth. "Goddammit!" he said angrily. "How we going to cook up some grub?"

"We're not," Frank replied curtly. "You know better'n to risk a fire." He turned to Kate. "Cold biscuits—and some dried meat. Maybe a little canned fruit."

She nodded and began to lay out the items. Neff swore again, deeply. Peck, rolling a wheat-straw cigarette, regarded the Army man with no particular interest. He struck a match, shielding it well with his hands; lit the smoke; and glanced at Sanderson.

"You worried about them four jaspers that was tailing us?"

Frank squatted on his heels. "Not them so much. Could be they weren't even interested—just happened to be out there. It's the others. They're moving straight in on us."

"Could be they're just happening along too."

Somewhere in the closing darkness, an owl hooted. Sanderson listened for a few moments, then said, "There's a difference. Why would they be coming up this side of the mountains?"

"Reckon you're right," the gunman murmured, and he studied the tip of his cigarette.

"It's ready," Kate called in a spiritless voice. "You can help yourselves."

Neff, still grumbling, crossed to where she had laid out the meal. Peck rose, pinched out the coal of his smoke, and followed. Sanderson watched Kate London move off toward her blanket roll. She met his gaze and shook her head.

"I'm too tired to eat."

"Were all tired," he said. "Eat anyway."

"I'm not hungry. I couldn't—"

He was too beat for patience. "Tomorrow'll be as bad as today," he said harshly. "Worse, if we have to make a run for it—and I won't be bothered by you being too weak to stay on your horse. Eat something."

She had the strength to flash him an angry look, then turned to the food. Taking two biscuits, a bit of the meat, and her canteen, she retired to her bed. Sanderson helped himself to enough food for his own needs, then left the clearing and climbed to the top of the nearest hill. Finding a flat rock, he sat down and began to munch on the stringy beef and dry bread.

The last of the flaring, gold light of day had gone. To the west the horizon lay in deep purple, shading to near black at its farthest points. About him the sounds of night were rising, and a faint breeze had begun to blow. But these things held little interest for Frank Sanderson. His eyes, aching dully from the long contest with the burning glare of the flats and hills, searched carefully across the shadowy land for tell-tale signs of their pursuers.

There was nothing. The stars appeared, then gradually bloomed to brighter intensity, and the world became a ghostly, silvered universe, hushed and eerie in its composition. To all intents and purposes, he and those of his party were the only trespassers in a silent void. But that, he knew, was false.

Those were not mirages he had seen that day to the south, nor were they spinning dust devils born of the heat and winds. Riders had created those yellowish spirals—men who at that moment were closing in steadily or, like him, had halted for the night and, employing the same care, built a fireless camp. Most likely, he concluded, the latter was true.

Both men and horses have their limit of endurance, and whoever had caused the dust clouds—assuming they too had left Whiterock that morning—would have been forced to halt. Taking comfort from that logic, Sanderson rose, spat out the last mouthful of tasteless meat and returned to camp. After quenching his thirst, he crawled stiffly into his blankets.

They were up before daylight, partook of a cold breakfast, and rode on, pointing directly north now for the rugged, bulking Peloncillos, now definite in form.

At the first opportunity, Sanderson climbed to the crest of a butte and, with sunlight flooding the land, made a careful study of their surroundings. There was no sign of the four riders to the east, but to the south a faint trickle of dust again hung in the sky. Wondering at that, he swung back and rejoined the others.

Kate looked at him anxiously, her question

voiceless.

"We shook that bunch that was behind us," he said. "Still somebody below. One party."

Peck, overhearing, frowned. "Was two yesterday. Think they've thrown in together?"

"Possible. Or else one bunch kept going until they reached the hills—the far end of where we were last night. Rocky country. There'd be no dust."

"If that's so," Kate London said slowly, "they're not far back."

"Ten miles, more or less."

There was a long silence. Finally Neff said, "We'll, if they are, they'll spot us sure. Nothing ahead but flats."

"And we'll spot them—works both ways," Frank said. He thought for a moment, then added, "Guess we ought to change this up a bit. You and Kate move on. Take the mules with you. Virg and I'll drop back a piece so's we can keep an eye on things."

The Army man nodded. "We just keep riding north?"

"Straight for the mountains," Sanderson said. He shifted his attention to Kate. "Where in the Peloncillos did your husband hide the gold?"

"The north end," she replied; then she stopped. Apparently she was weighing the advisability of being more specific, then decided it was necessary. "Place he called Calaveras Canyon. We can find it by the two peaks—one on each side, like a gate."

"Know where it is," Sanderson said. "Indian country."

Virgil Peck's eyes flickered. "Apaches?"

"Chiricahuas. Seems they've always figured that part of the mountain their private territory. Sacred ground, I guess. We won't have any trouble if we're careful. Thing to watch out for is young bucks looking to blood themselves— and renegades." Sanderson motioned to Neff. "Move on, but if you see us cutting away, stop. Best we don't get strung out too much."

Harvey Neff took command at once and shortly thereafter, with Kate at his side and the pack animals trailing behind, rode off.

Frank and Virgil Peck watched them depart. When they had reached a point a quarter mile ahead, the two men resumed the journey.

"We stay like this or wing out?" Peck asked.

"No need to split up yet. Once we get closer to the mountain, it'll be a good idea."

The morning wore on, with the heat increasing steadily. They were again on a broad mesa, a flat, treeless stretch that linked the first upthrust of low hills, where they had made camp the previous night, to the Peloncillos. It was little different from the desert itself, and soon they fell into the customary pattern of riding for an hour, then resting the horses for fifteen minutes.

Near midafternoon, Sanderson forged ahead and caught up with the rest of the party. He motioned toward a long strip of dark growth

38

jutting from the near end of the jumbled range.

"Bear Springs," he said, his voice almost a croak.

"Camp there tonight."

Neff moved his head up and down. Kate London stirred wearily. Frank gave her a closer look. She had tired more quickly than she had the previous day. Her face was dust-streaked, and she had opened the top buttons of her shirt, exposing her neck in search of relief from the heat. The skin had turned bright red.

"You're getting a bad burn," he said.

She began to close the blouse, doing it spiritlessly. He smiled sympathetically. "It'll be cool at the spring. And we've got the worst of it behind us."

"I'm all right," she murmured as he wheeled away. He rested the chestnut until Peck drew alongside. "Be damn glad when that sun's down," he said, mopping at his eyes with the back of a hand. "See anything?"

Virg grunted. "Nothing but sand and rocks. A gila monster wouldn't stay in this country." He jerked his thumb toward the south. "Company's still coming."

Sanderson squinted into the glare. The riders had neither gained nor lost ground—were simply holding their distance. "Not wanting to catch up," he said. "Not yet."

"Seems," the gunman said. "How's the lady doing?"

"Plenty beat, but she's game. Quite a

woman."

"For sure."

"We'll have a decent camp tonight. Give her a chance to rest up."

"Something we'll all be needing, maybe."

Sanderson swung a questioning glance to Peck.

"That mean something?"

"Been thinking about the Apaches. They can smell a white man coming ten miles off."

Frank shrugged. "Likely won't run into any this far south. If they jump us, it'll be around Calaveras Canyon."

Peck's face was a grim mask. "Just as soon we'd miss them completely. One thing I sure don't like is Apaches."

"Why? Have some trouble with them?"

The little gunman squirmed on his saddle. "Plenty. Bunch of them grabbed me and a couple of boys over Silver City way a few years back. Put us through holy hell. Used knives and everything else they could rustle up—then staked us out on ant hills."

"They know all the cute tricks," Sanderson agreed.

"Wasn't nothing they forgot. But I got lucky. Worked myself loose. Hid in one of the wicki-ups until I got a chance to steal a horse and run for it."

Sanderson made no comment. Peck was staring into the distance, his voice low and taut.

"Still hear them boys yelling while the ants

worked them over. Made up my mind a long time ago them redskins'd never take me again—alive."

Frank studied Virgil Peck quietly. This was a side of the gunman he had never before seen. After a time, he said, "Don't stew over it. We move in careful, we won't draw any attention. I figure our trouble's coming from outsiders—from whoever's trailing us. They heard London spouting off about all that gold he found and buried, and now they're after it."

"That kind of trouble I don't mind. Stand my ground against any man living. But Apaches—"

Sanderson was silent. Fear was something he had never associated with Virg Peck. It just went to prove, he guessed, that every man had a soft spot.

They reached Bear Springs at nightfall and made camp along the short stream that bubbled forth from beneath a ledge of rock, meandered lazily through the cottonwoods and brush for a few hundred feet, and disappeared again into the thirsty earth.

The pleasant coolness was a vast relief from the blistering eye of the sun, and everyone began to feet better quickly. They had an enjoyable meal, cooked by Kate, and when that was over, preparations for the night were made.

Frank Sanderson, however, felt himself far from sleep. After laying out his blankets, he rose, crossed to the horses, and began throwing his gear onto the chestnut. Peck, indulging himself in a final smoke, looked up.

"Where you heading for?"

"Figured to have a look at who's trailing us."

"Want me along?"

"No need. Keep that fire low."

Harvey Neff, sitting on his blankets, said, "Yes, sir, General," and waved a half-empty bottle of whiskey at Sanderson. "How about a nip of snake-bite medicine? Mighty good for aching bones."

"Save it for the snake bites," Frank replied, and mounting up, he rode off into the night.

He cut wide of the trail they had followed, choosing instead the rougher ground to the west. He had no real reason to make a ride into the silver-shot darkness other than to satisfy curiosity, and perhaps allay a feeling that there was even more to Kate London's supposedly simple excursion into the Peloncillos after gold rightfully hers than he had been led to believe.

She had failed to mention that her husband had spread word of his find all the way from the mountains to El Paso; and she had not divulged the location of the treasure until the last possible moment. All of that disturbed him, left him at loose ends. Was there more she was keeping secret?

Uneasy, he rode on. Near the edge of the trees, he heard a sound off to his right and halted to listen. When it did not come again, he decided it likely was an animal startled by his passage and went on. He broke free of the growth and came again onto the barren mesa. The night was bright, and he realized he offered an easy target to anyone so inclined, but there was small risk: Those who trailed them would make no move until the gold was located.

Three miles below the spring, he thought he saw the glint of a campfire and worked his way toward it, only to discover he had been mistaken. It was the reflection of moonlight upon a slab of mica.

He started a broad circle then, intending to cut back to camp on the opposite side of the trail. The nearby stamp of a horse brought him up short. Hunched on the saddle, nerves taut, he waited for the sound to come again.

CHAPTER SEVEN

Harvey Neff watched Sanderson ride off into the brush. A dull anger, prodded relentlessly by the liquor he had consumed, was building within him. Over to his left Peck had again stretched out in his blankets, grunting wearily as he sought comfort on the hard ground. Kate London, apparently, was already asleep.

He pulled himself to his feet impatiently and, staggering a bit, walked a short distance into the shadows. There he sat down, back to a stump, his mind dark and seething. That goddam Sanderson—what the hell was the matter with him? You'd think nobody but him had any sense. Anybody'd know better'n build up the fire at a time like this.

It wasn't the fool command so much, he told himself, taking a long pull at the bottle; it was the idea behind it—the implication on Sanderson's part that he was the hot-shot ramrod, that he knew everything. And he was getting worse.

"Ain't you turning in?" Peck called sleepily from the edge of the firelight.

"Aim to set here for a spell," Neff replied. He had been sore beat when they arrived at the spring, but now, after the meal and most of the quart of whiskey, he was feeling much more alive.

He watched Virg Peck settle back into his bed and almost at once begin to snore. A bit of pitch-laden wood snapped in the fire, exploding a small roll of smoke that surged upward. Far back up on the slope a coyote barked. A quick reply came from a more distant point.

Could be Apaches, the Army man thought. Sanderson had said they were moving into Indian country. Sanderson! Fresh anger moved through him. Goddammit, it was always Sanderson. They even had him doing it. And who had given him leave to take over, anyway? He was nothing but a two-bit lawman from a two-bit hick town.

He'd never been anybody big. He was like the Army brass—always throwing their weight around, telling everybody do this, do that, when

44

two-thirds of the time they didn't know what it was all about. Harvey Neff's jumbling thoughts came to a halt. Kate London had brushed aside her blankets and now was standing upright. She glanced at Peck, then toward his own bed. Evidently she did not see him there in the shadows. As he watched, she turned and, with a towel over her shoulder, walked hurriedly toward the pool below the spring.

Secret pleasure stirred Neff. Kate was going to have herself a bath. He tipped the bottle to his lips again as an oily shine appeared on his cheeks and forehead. Evidently Kate had delayed until she thought they were all asleep—all but Sanderson. Damn Sanderson! And damn her! She didn't mind that he was somewhere around while she stripped off and played around in the water.

He remained motionless for several minutes, brooding over that conclusion and then, freshly angered by such injustice, he emptied the whiskey bottle, tossed it away, and got to his feet. Dropping back into the brush, he circled the camp and headed for the lower end of the pool. He had some rights too—same as Sanderson— same as everybody else.

Before he saw Kate he heard her moving about in the water, splashing quietly, humming a low tune. He discovered he could not get down to the pool at that point because of a rocky ledge, and once again he cut back and swung wide. When he came again to the water

45

she had finished her bathing and had climbed onto the sandy bank. Dressed in some sort of robe, she sat on a log drying her hair with the towel.

He watched her hungrily for a time while the fever in his blood mounted and then, unable to control himself, plunged into the clearing and staggered toward her. She heard him and sprang to her feet.

"You!" she exclaimed, recognizing him. "Thought for a moment—"

"That it was Sanderson—that it?"

She regarded him with a steady gaze. "Matter of fact, I was thinking of the Apaches."

"Sure, sure," he said, moving in nearer. "I'll just bet on it."

Kate continued to stare at his slack face. After a bit she began to collect her belongings and started to turn for the camp. Instantly he lunged, caught her by the shoulders, and whirled her roughly.

"What's the matter?" he demanded, his face close to hers. "Ain't I good enough for you?"

"You're drunk," she said, trying to push him away.

He released her shoulders and wrapped his arms about her body. "Now, what's wrong with being a little drunk?" he asked thickly. "Maybe, was I to go get another bottle—"

Kate managed to pull back and partly free herself. She slapped him smartly across the face. His eyes flamed as fury overrode all else.

46

"Goddamn you—don't play cozy with me!" he rasped and began to force her backward. "Don't fool me none—them high-and-mighty airs! Seen your kind before. You got to be horsed around."

She struggled to get clear of him, lashing out with her fists, kicking with her feet, fighting with a silent, desperate intensity. But she was no match for his strength. Slowly, he bore her down.

Exultation roared through him, and then he was aware of the hard pressure of a gun barrel digging into his middle. She had managed somehow to draw his pistol and turn it against him. He tried to pull away, then felt shocking, searing pain rip through him as a muffled blast hurled him to one side. And then, for Harvey Neff, the world ceased to exist.

CHAPTER EIGHT

Frank Sanderson strained into the starlit night. The sound had come from somewhere directly ahead—but only the empty, flat surface of the mesa lay before him. He stalled out a long minute...another. Again he heard the dull thud of a hoof, this time followed by the faint jingle of bridle metal.

Frowning, he put the chestnut to a slow walk, his eyes probing restlessly. Suddenly the land fell away from him, dropped off into a wide coulee fifteen or twenty feet deep. He stopped instantly, surprised at the discovery. He had thought the mesa unbroken; he understood now *why* he had had difficulty in pegging the sound.

Dismounting, he made his way to where he could look into the depression. Three horses stood in the low brush to his left, little more than vague outlines in the shadows. At first he saw no riders. He located them finally squatting on their heels at the foot of a small butte. While he watched, a match flared in the darkness as one lit a cigarette. The distance was too great to make recognition possible.

Returning to the gelding, he continued a circuit of the hollow, eyes now on the soft sand as he searched for hoofprints. He found them a short time later, leading in from the south. Sanderson grunted in satisfaction. This would be one of the parties that had been trailing them.

Abandoning all efforts toward silence, he hawked noisily, spat, wheeled the chestnut about, and rode straight into the coulee. When he reached the floor of the basin, the men were standing. They faced him, two with rifles slung in the crook of their elbows.

"Çomo esta, señor?"

At the greeting, Sanderson halted. All of the men were Mexicans. Grinning, he said, "Howdy. Didn't expect to find anybody camped here. You run out of matches?"

The tallest of the trio cocked his head to one

48

side.

Light played on the silver ornaments decorating his clothing and glowed dully against his swarthy skin.

"I do not understand, *señor.*"

"Man usually builds a fire when he makes camp—unless he's hiding from somebody."

The Mexican laughed quietly. "When there is no food for cooking, there is no need for fire. Where do you go?"

There had been no invitation to dismount, a courtesy ordinarily extended travelers. Ignoring that, Frank swung his leg over the saddle and dropped to the ground. He wanted a closer look at the men. There was something familiar about them.

"North," he said, squaring around until he faced them. "And you?"

"We ride east—to New Mexico. We hear of much cattle work in the Cimarron country."

The tall Mexican was lying in his teeth, and the awareness of that increased the anger in Sanderson. He looked them over carefully. All were dressed much alike: ornate cloth jackets, tight breeches, collarless shirts, wide-brimmed *sombreros.* But they were not *ordinary vaqueros;* these were tough, hard-eyed men with an arrogance to their bearing. Suddenly it dawned ·on *him,* and he knew why they had appeared familiar; they were Rurales, members of the Mexican military.

Masking surprise, Sanderson hooked his

49

thumbs in his belt and glanced up at the velvet black sky with its silver studs. "Fine night for traveling. Where'd you come from?"

The tall man moved his hand in an indefinite wave toward the west. "Arizona." In the pale light, his cheek bones looked high and the aquiline curve of his nose more pronounced.

Sanderson's right hand slid imperceptibly to the cedar pistol at his hip, coming to rest on the worn cedar handle.

"You're a poor liar, *amigo*," he said quietly. "Tracks show you came in from the south. And you're sure as hell not cowpunchers. I figure you for Rurales."

The tan man stiffened, then eased off. "It is for you to believe what you wish."

"I believe what I see," Sanderson snapped. "Tell your men to drop their rifles. Were going to talk."

The Mexican gave an order in Spanish. He watched the weapons fall and for several moments held his eyes on them. Finally he looked up.

"Are we to have trouble, *señor?*"

"Up to you. I'm asking for some straight answers. First off, Sergeant, what are Rurales doing this far north of the border? Seems I recall an agreement our governments have about not crossing over."

"Captain," the Mexican corrected politely. "Captain Pablo Mendoza—at your service."

"All right—Captain. What are you doing

50

here?"

Mendoza moved his shoulders. "It is not uncommon for us to seek bandits that have crossed the line. Your country also is guilty of such."

"Maybe. Who're you looking for?" The officer lifted his hands, then allowed them to fall. "Names are of no importance. And of *bandidos* there are always plenty."

Mendoza was hedging. Anger and suspicion mounted higher within Frank Sanderson.

"That's no answer! Maybe you think I don't know you've been dogging my tracks for two days. Why?"

Mendoza appeared astonished. "I, *señor?* You I have never before seen. Why should I follow you?"

"I'm asking you that, Captain."

"We do not trail you. Perhaps I was not with truth in the beginning, but—"

"Watched your dust coming up behind me and my party. Then you make a cold camp here—just a few miles below us. Got to be a reason. I want to hear it."

One of the soldiers said something. Mendoza nodded. "You are camped ahead—at the spring, perhaps?"

"You know that. Somebody with me you're interested in? That why you're tagging us?"

"I do not know who rides with you. How could I say—"

The distant report of a gunshot cut through

Mendoza's words. Sanderson went taut and glanced to the north. The shot could have come from the spring—or it could have been farther east. It sounded muffled—possibly because of remote origin. Uneasy, he swung back to the officer.

"I've got a woman by the name of London with me. Kate London. Two men—one called Virgil Peck, another known as Harvey Neff. I'm Frank Sanderson. Now—who're you looking for?"

"All are strangers."

"Then why the hell are you trailing us?" Sanderson demanded, exasperated and not a little worried.

"I do not, *señor*. This I assure you."

The urgency to return to camp now hammering at him, Frank faced the Rurale captain. "I'm not believing that, Mendoza—but I can't stand here and argue about it. This is big country, and tomorrow when you pull out, pick yourself another trail. That clear?"

The Mexican dipped his head, smiling blandly. "Of course, *señor*. I wish no trouble."

Frank stepped back to the gelding and hoisted himself to the saddle.

"You'll get it if I see your dust behind us in the morning," he said, and whipping about, he rushed off into the night.

CHAPTER NINE

Anxiety riding him with sharpened spurs, Frank Sanderson hurried on through the darkness. He was convinced now that there was more to the expedition than Kate London had admitted, and the thought that he had been taken in by the cool, quiet-faced woman galled him. And Mendoza had something to do with it—he was sure of that. But what?

As he drew nearer the camp, his thoughts shifted and caution laid its restraint upon him. That gunshot—it could have come from the Springs. It was best he proceed with care. Neff or Virgil Peck would not have fired—if one of them had—had there not been good reason.

He reached the first scatter of trees and brush and approached slowly, winding in and out of the growth. He saw Kate London first of all, standing just beyond the fire. Farther over in the half-darkness he saw the body of Harvey Neff stretched out on the ground. Nearby, Peck was hollowing out a grave in the sandy soil. Sanderson held back no longer. He roweled the gelding sharply and entered the clearing at a gallop.

"What happened here?" he shouted, leaving the saddle fast.

Peck ceased his digging. Kate faced Sanderson. "I killed him."

"You killed him!" he echoed. "In the name of God, why?"

Peck dropped his short-handled spade and walked into the center of the clearing. He ducked his head at Kate. "She went down to the creek. Guess Harvey got all worked up; he followed her. Was pretty drunk."

Sanderson swore. "You have to kill him?"

Kate London nodded. "I did," she said calmly. "We can go on without him. Drunk's good for nobody."

"He could use a gun—and that's what counted. Way this is shaping up, three of us won't be enough. Now, with only two—"

"I can hold up my end," she broke in.

Anger pushed through Sanderson. "Seems you can do plenty—and right now I want some truth out of you. I want the whole goddam story about that gold your husband buried!"

Kate stiffened. "I've told you—"

"Not all of it—and if I don't get it quick, I'm dropping the whole thing in your lap and pulling out."

"You know all there is that—"

"I know just about what you want me to. If I knew it all, then I wouldn't be wondering why three Mexican Rurales are trailing us."

"Mexican—soldiers? I—I don't know why—"

"You do," Frank said, his voice low. "Now, do you talk or do we call it quits?"

Kate stared at the tall lawman for a long minute. Finally she shrugged. "I didn't think it was

54

important—I mean, all the other things."

"I'll decide if they are."

She hesitated and looked toward Neff. "Hadn't we better—"

"Waiting won't bother him. Go ahead—talk."

Kate moved nearer the fire and sat down on a log.

"The treasure," she said, her gaze lost in the low flames, "is all in gold coin."

Sanderson drew to attention. That accounted for the presence of Mendoza and his men. The Mexican authorities had sent them to recover the gold, probably stolen from some bank—or possibly the government itself. He cursed himself silently for getting mixed up in such an affair.

"It wasn't stolen by Dan," Kate said, as if reading his mind. "It was being smuggled to Tucson—at least, that's what my husband figured, although he couldn't understand why the mule train had come so far north."

The reason was clear: Whoever was heading up the train had wanted to avoid Skeleton Canyon. There were always plenty of outlaws in that particular area. But Sanderson said nothing, merely waited.

"Dan was in the Peloncillos looking for a lost silver mine," Kate London continued. "Someone had sold him a map that supposedly would take him to the exact place where there was a lot of rich ore. One morning he saw a pack train down below, following the trail at the foot of the mountain. He knew they were Mexicans from the clothing they wore. A dozen or so men, he said, and as many pack mules.

"About the time he caught sight of them, a party of Apaches attacked. There were twenty or thirty of them—all with rifles. It was a massacre. The men the Indians didn't kill outright, they spent the day torturing. Late in the afternoon, after the last Mexican was dead, they unloaded the mules and hid the things the smugglers had been hauling in a cave. Then they left—taking the mules."

"Apaches got a tooth for mule meat," Peck commented. "Like it better than anything."

"While they were gone," Kate said, not hearing, "Dan went into the cave. There was a lot of stuff there, but the big thing was the gold. Four chests, all filled with coins. He knew the Apaches had little use for it and likely wouldn't care if it just disappeared. So he took the chests, one by one, and started moving them back into the canyon—Calaveras Canyon. He had to carry them himself ; it was too rough for a horse.

"He got three of the chests moved and was after the fourth when several of the Indians showed up. There was a fight, and he killed most of them—but he got shot too, and barely escaped. The rest you know."

Frank shook his head and threw a glance at Peck. "Means we've not only got the Rurales and every outlaw who bumped into London on our backs, but the Apaches too."

"Apaches?" Kate said, frowning. "They won't be any trouble. Treasure means nothing to them."

"Maybe not—but they'll be plenty riled over those braves your husband killed. They'll figure he'll come back for that fourth chest of gold. They'll sit tight and wait."

"But he's dead!"

"How would they know that?" Frank said impatiently. "They'll lay for the first white man coming into Calaveras Canyon."

"It's been several weeks. Isn't it possible they've forgotten?"

"Indians don't forget—and they've got nothing else but time. Anyway, if we managed somehow to get by them, there's still Mendoza, and his Rurales—and maybe a few outlaws."

Kate rose to her feet. "Makes no difference," she said. "The gold's mine. My husband paid for it with his life. I intend to get it—for my daughter—and myself."

Sanderson studied her thoughtfully. She was a determined woman; also a foolish one. "Take my advice," he said. "Forget it. Odds are all against you."

"But worth the gamble," she came back instantly.

"And I'm reminding you—both of you—I have your word that you'll see it through."

The lawman's eyes narrowed. "Room for argument there. I gave you my word, same as Peck and Neff, but you never got around to laying the truth on the line. You told us just enough to get us started."

"Doesn't change anything," she said stubbornly. "You still made a promise."

Sanderson shrugged and stared off into the shadowy night to hide the anger that tore at him. Against such feminine logic he could find no defense—and he was now convinced their chance of recovering London's treasure and getting out alive was nil.

"All right," he said after a time. "I gave my word. I'll stand by it."

"Good," she said, some of the edge leaving her voice. "And to make it better for you, I'll split Neff's share of the money between you—five hundred apiece."

Virgil Peck snorted. "Money ain't much good to a dead man," he said drily.

She smiled and made an off-hand gesture. "I don't think it's as bad as you believe. It'll all turn out."

Peck stared, spat, then turned away. Sanderson shifted wearily.

"Have it your way," he said. For a long moment his eyes remained fixed on Harvey Neff's body, and then he added, "Let's get him buried and move on. No point in making it easy for Mendoza."

CHAPTER TEN

They buried Harvey Neff, piled stones high upon his grave to keep coyotes and other animals from disturbing the body, released his sorrel horse to let it fend for itself, and pushed on. They traveled ten miles farther west and made a new camp on a rocky slope at the lower end of the Peloncillos.

Before daylight the next morning they had mounted and were striking due north, keeping the long, ragged chain of peaks and canyons to their left. Sanderson took the precaution of staying well within the fringe of brush and rock along the foot of the mountain. It was slower going, and the horses labored, but the lawmen deemed it wise to screen their movements.

All doubt of pursuit was gone from his mind now. Somewhere behind them, Mendoza and his men would be searching the hills and flats for them. The dust clouds they had noticed those previous days indicated others—unknown parties yet to show themselves.

And ahead were the Apaches.

They were a patient people when it came to avenging their kin. Grim, deadly, they would keep a closer watch on Calaveras Canyon, where the killings had taken place—and wait. They well knew the white man's craze for *Peshklitso*—the yellow iron he would rob and murder to possess. It would bring the killer back to them. They would be ready.

It was the Apaches who presented the greatest threat, Sanderson thought, as they toiled across a long slope. Given a little luck they might outsmart Mendoza and the others, but the painted warriors were a different matter.

He could figure only on Peck and himself if it came down to an attack—and he wasn't too sure of Peck where the Apaches were concerned. Kate had strapped on Neff's gun belt, was wearing it as a man would, but whether she could use the weapon was problematical. He swore quietly. Losing Harvey Neff put them in a bad position. If she hadn't been so damned hasty...

Suddenly tired of thinking about it, Sanderson swung his eyes to Kate London, recalling in that moment her mention of a daughter. It seemed odd that she could be a mother—she was not the type, and a man didn't expect it to be so. He eased the sweating chestnut nearer to her horse. She turned her face to him questioningly.

"That daughter you spoke of—she live in El Paso too?"

Her cool reserve stood between them like a barrier. "I don't see that it concerns you—but no, she doesn't."

"Could concern me," he said curtly, aroused by her antagonism. "If you don't make it back, and I do, I'll need to know where to deliver your share."

Her manner relented perceptibly. "I'm sorry. I thought you were being curious. She's in San Antonio—in a convent."

"Name?"

"Marguerite Beaumont."

Sanderson frowned. "Not London?"

"No. Her father was Dandy Beaumont."

He repeated the name. "Sounds familiar. Could be I've heard of him."

"You would have if you ever sailed the Mississippi. He was a riverboat gambler. Dead now."

Frank continued to sift the information through his memory, but could not pin it down. At length he asked, "In which convent at San Antonio?"

"One run by some nuns called the Sisters of Sorrow. I put her there not long after Dandy was shot. I couldn't raise her, not with the kind of jobs I had to take."

"Lots of women manage."

"Not if they want their daughters reared the way I wanted mine to be. She'll never know the kind of life I was forced to lead."

"That means she doesn't know you work in a saloon?"

"She doesn't know anything about me," Kate said with a heavy sigh. "We haven't seen each other since the day I left her at the convent. I told them to keep her until I returned—and I made up my mind I wouldn't do that until I could care for her properly."

Sanderson's eyes were on a golden eagle soaring effortlessly above the peaks, dipping and wheeling in wide, graceful arcs.

"How long ago was that?"

"Thirteen—almost fourteen years. She's near seventeen now."

He looked at her wonderingly. "You sure she's still there?"

It was Kate's turn to register surprise. "Of course! Why wouldn't she be? I told the nuns to keep her until I came back. I've sent money for her needs from time to time. There's no reason why she won't be."

He shrugged. "Kids grow up—and they grow a mind of their own while they're doing it. She the big reason why you're so set on finding that gold?"

"The only one. Marguerite's going to be somebody. I'll take her east—away from this country. She'll never learn about my life—what I've had to do to keep alive."

His gaze was again on the eagle, now plummeting earthward in pursuit of some luckless prey. "Doubt if she'd be ashamed of you. Children have a way of understanding things—more than we give them credit for. You probably don't need to fret over it."

She smiled, brushing at the small beads of sweat on her forehead. "Perhaps, but I can't risk it. I don't want her ever to know. I just want to drive up in a fancy carriage some day, take her away to a decent life—try to make up for all the years she's been without a mother."

He was seeing a different Kate London, Frank realized; a Kate who was subdued, almost sad, and somewhat uncertain.

"It'll work out," he said kindly. "Maybe your Marguerite did have a rough go of it, but she can be proud of her mother. You had it worse."

Kate gave him a quiet smile. "I hope so—but it's been so long now. She doesn't even know I'm alive."

"She does if you've been sending money."

"I'm afraid that wasn't very often. There was never much to spare. Dan was always needing cash, and I had to live. It's been three years, at least."

"Kids do a lot of hoping," Sanderson said, easing himself on the saddle. "She'll be no exception. Be a fine thing if we can pull this off and make all her dreams—and yours—come true."

Kate looked at him soberly. "I—I have to, Frank. I can't fail her again."

"Might as well make that we," he grinned. "We're all wrapped up in this together."

Touching the brim of his hat, he pulled away, striking up the slope until he was on higher ground. Halting, he flung his glance out onto the glittering flats. Far to the southeast, three dots moved slowly toward the end of the mountain. There was no distinction at such a distance, but he knew instantly it could be only

Pablo Mendoza and his soldiers.

He studied them intently. He had known his threats would not turn the Mexicans back, that he should be satisfied that his moving the camp during the night had afforded them a substantial lead. But he still did not like what he saw. Mendoza was an expert; he had discovered quickly what had taken place and was coming on. He would be difficult to shake.

There was a smaller dust roll farther east— almost to the foot of the mountain. Riders, un-questionably, but they were hidden from view and he could not determine their number. More vultures rushing to get in on the spoils. All were too distant, however, to pose any immediate threat.

His glance moved on, sweeping the endless flats and the low, bubble-like hills, finally reaching the towering ridges and peaks of the mountain itself. He came to sudden attention. Smoke, in a thin, twisting column of gray, was lifting upward from one of the jutting ledges, laying a signal in the cloudless sky.

Sanderson swore savagely. The Indians had spotted them and were passing along the warning. From that moment on they would be under constant watch. It was a piece of bad luck; he had hoped to reach Calaveras Canyon before drawing their attention.

Disturbed, he returned to the others, still laboring tediously over the rutted trail. He said nothing about the smoke signal, and since none of them mentioned it he assumed it had gone unnoticed. Grim, he fell in line with the procession, and the breathlessly hot day dragged on.

Near sundown he called a halt in a cluster of scrub oak. The animals needed rest, and the thick brush offered an ideal place in which to spend the night and not advertise their exact position. It was useless now, however, to try to hide from the Apaches.

They set up a camp, watered the horses and mules from the canteens, and picketed them on a thin stand of grass struggling for survival around the banks of a dead spring. Once there had been water in the hollow, but like all such sources, it became dry periodically—all depending upon the preceding winter. Since the sand was loose and powdery for a considerable depth, Sanderson reckoned there had been little snow on that side of the Peloncillos for years.

Later, as they sat around the low fire drinking coffee and taking pleasure in the coolness that had set in, Sanderson glanced at Kate. "We're close to Calaveras Canyon. Ought to be there by midmorning."

Her face brightened. "Will it be hard to find?"

"No trouble. Rough country, though. Be lucky if we don't lose a horse or a mule."

He paused, eyes on the dark fringe of brush that encircled the camp as small warnings of danger plucked at his consciousness. He had seen movement, heard a slight sound—whether animal or human he could not be sure. Casually he lowered the tin cup he was holding and placed it on the ground beside him. His hand settled on the butt of his pistol. Virgil Peck, missing none of this, followed suit.

Kate London looked from one to the other, suddenly aware of the tension. "What is it?" she asked in a whisper.

"Don't move," Frank murmured. "Something—or somebody's—out there."

At that precise moment the long, narrow head of a horse broke into the fire's glare. The animal halted abruptly. A man, doubled forward over the saddle, swayed uncertainly and then fell heavily to the sand.

CHAPTER ELEVEN

For the space of a dozen breaths no one moved, and then Frank Sanderson leaped to his feet. He strode across the small clearing to where the man sprawled. Peck, not one to trust the unexpected, took up a position slightly to one side, pistol in hand. Kate London hurried after the lawman.

As Sanderson knelt over the rider, she asked, "Do you know him?"

He shook his head. The stranger was young—in his early twenties. He had dark, curly hair; a clean-shaven, boyish face. His clothing was covered by dust, and the heels of his scarred boots were badly run over. He wore a pistol and a knife at his waist.

"Hasn't been shot," Sanderson said, frowning. He glanced at Peck. "Bring some water, Virg. Maybe that'll bring him to."

The gunman complied. Frank raised the pilgrim's head, pressed the rim of the tin cup to his lips, and forced a quantity of liquid into his mouth. The boy choked, swallowed, then gulped the remainder of the water eagerly.

He brushed at his eyes and stared at Sanderson. His glanced shifted and took in Kate and Peck. "The Indians—they gone?"

The lawman frowned. "Apaches after you?"

"Been dodging them for two whole days."

A note of despair slipped from Kate London's lips. "Means they've found us too. You've—you've led them here."

Sanderson turned to Peck. "Take a look. See if there's any sign..."

The gunman did not stir for a moment. Then, reluctantly, he moved by the newcomer's buckskin horse and disappeared into the brush. Frank watched him go, then returned to the boy, now struggling to a sitting position.

"Name's Farr—Billy Farr," he said, mustering a grin. "Plumb sorry to come busting in on you like this. Don't want to cause you no trouble."

"It's all right," Kate replied in a tired voice. "I'm sorry too—for what I said."

"I understand. Got no business dragging my problems to your door. Didn't mean to, actually. Reckon it just happened."

"Where'd the Apaches jump you?" Sanderson asked, rising. He extended his hand to assist Farr, who got up quickly.

"Yonder side of the mountain. Been running and hiding ever since. Thought they had me for sure once or twice. Guess I was just plain lucky." Farr glanced longingly at the fire. "It all right if I help myself to some of that coffee? Smells mighty good."

"Of course," Kate said, and crossing back she poured him a cup of the strong, black liquid.

Sanderson studied Billy Farr through half-closed eyes. "You do something to put the Apaches on your back?"

Billy shook his head. "Nope—nothing. Beats me what riled them—unless it's just that I'm a white man."

Peck appeared at the edge of the camp. "Nobody out there. No sign."

Frank nodded. Moving to where Farr's buckskin waited, he examined the horse briefly, then led it to where the other animals were picketed. As he turned back to the fire, he heard Kate speak.

"Where are you from, Billy?"

"Lots of places, ma'am. Right now I was riding up from Nogales, headed for Santa Fe." Farr paused to sip his coffee. "But I ain't particular. I'm just hunting a job."

68

Kate glanced at Sanderson, then to Billy. "Maybe we could hire you on. Can you handle a gun?"

Farr grinned broadly. "Well, thank you, ma'am! I'd really be obliged. Being broke ain't no fun. And I can use a gun—knife, too—good as the next man, I expect."

Kate London again looked to Sanderson. "It agreeable to you?"

The lawman had halted directly in front of Farr. "No, it's not," he said bluntly. "Leastwise, not until I hear the truth."

Kate stared at him, startled. Billy Farr's features hardened for a fleeting moment; then he turned away.

"Don't know what you mean," he mumbled.

"The hell you don't. This is all a show. You ride in here, fall off your horse like you were dead beat. Watching you, a man would think you've been on the run for days, and was having a bad time of it. I won't swallow that yarn."

"But, I—"

"Man only has to look close at you to know you're lying about the Apaches. Your horse won't prove out, either. Both of you'd be half dead if things were the way you claim."

Billy Farr squirmed uneasily. He placed his cup on a rock and stood with head hung low. Finally he shrugged.

"Might've known I'd never fool nobody, mister. Never was good at lying."

His voice was ragged in defeat. He raised his

69

eyes to Kate London. "I'm real sorry, ma'am—but I was scared. Was ready to try anything."

"Scared of what?" she asked.

"Of the Indians—the Apaches. They're out there, sure enough. Maybe they wasn't exactly chasing me, but they was watching every move I made. And being all alone, I reckon I plain lost my nerve. Got the feeling I just had to find me some white people."

Kate's features softened. She started to speak, but Sanderson silenced her with a gesture.

"Why didn't you just ride in, like any other pilgrim? Why all the fancy acting?"

"Was scared you wouldn't take me in. Figured if I made out like I was about gone, you'd let me stay with you all."

The lawman was unimpressed. "And this business about the Apaches?"

"Well, they ain't really looking for me," Farr said quickly. "Just sort of cooked that up."

"Then there's no reason why you can't keep on riding to Santa Fe, or wherever you're going."

Farr moaned softly, glanced fearfully toward the brush. "Was afraid you'd say that. Danged Indians purely give me the creeps."

"I think we should hire him," Kate said, taking a firm stand. "We need another man—one to take Neff's place."

"We need another gun," Sanderson corrected. "A half a dozen, if we could find them. But the way he feels about Apaches, I doubt if he'd be

70

much use to us."

The instant the words were out, Frank realized how they would sound to Virgil Peck. He glanced at the gunman. Peck was staring into the fire. If he had heard, he gave no indication.

"You mean fighting them?" Farr asked. "That what you're talking about? Shucks, don't worry none about that. I'd be fine, was I along with somebody like you. It's being alone that devils me."

"If they jump us," Sanderson said drily, "they'll likely be so plentiful you'll think you're alone."

"Still wouldn't fret me none. Be a cinch standing up to them with men like you. I figure we could hold our own against two, maybe three times as many Indians."

"You don't know much about the Apaches," Peck commented, rousing.

"Maybe I don't, but I'm sure willing to take my chances with you two fellers."

"You're hired," Kate London said, flatly and decisively. She raised her eyes to Sanderson, "We'll need him. I'll pay him myself."

Frank opened his mouth to speak, but thought better of it. He didn't feel right about Billy Farr, but it would mean one more gun. Squatting, he poured himself a measure of fresh coffee, only half listening as Billy made his profuse thanks to Kate.

"I'm sure obliged to you, ma'am. And don't you worry none. You won't be sorry you give

71

me a chance. Just what kind of a job am I getting?"

"We're here after gold. Some my husband hid for me. We may have trouble with the Indians and we may not. And there are others who are following us. They want it too."

Billy frowned. "If it's yours, what business have the Apaches and them others got trying to keep you from it?"

"It's a long story," Kate said, "and not important to you. I'll pay you five hundred dollars if we get the treasure out and make it back to El Paso."

Billy Farr's eyes spread. "Five hundred dollars!" he echoed in an incredulous voice. "Five hundred!"

"In gold. But you'd better understand this. You could lose your life."

Farr bobbed his head excitedly. "Makes no difference to me, ma'am! For that much money I'd crawl through a den of rattlesnakes!" He grinned and waved a hand at Sanderson and Virgil Peck. "But I reckon we ain't got much to worry about—not with them two."

The little gunman sighed heavily and looked at Frank. "Guess every man's got to be young once," he said wryly.

72

CHAPTER TWELVE

In the cold pre-dawn of the following morning they loaded the pack mules and made ready for the final lap to Calaveras Canyon.

Tight-lipped, Frank Sanderson considered what lay ahead. From the moment he had wormed the complete story of Dan London's treasure from a reluctant Kate, he had felt their chances for survival were very small. But he had pushed on, actuated by a ruthless sort of honor that had always dominated his life. He had given his word; he would see the thing through to a finish despite Apaches, outlaws, and the whole damned Mexican Army, if necessary.

The others were equally silent, except for Billy Farr, who went about the chores assigned him with a noisy whistling.

Peck, engaged in securing the load on one of the mules, scowled. "Cut out that racket," he snapped.

Farr hushed instantly and cast an injured look at the gunman. "Just being happy..."

"We can do without it," Peck said. "You better start learning right now."

"Someone's coming!"

Kate, a dozen paces away and already in the saddle, broke into Virgil's reply. "Just saw a man's head," she added.

Sanderson, alarm hammering through him,

stepped quickly to her side. "Where?"

She pointed down the slope to a narrow opening in the dense brush. "Between those clumps. Just a glimpse—a man on a horse."

"Not an Indian?"

"No—"

Abruptly another rider crossed, was there for a fraction of time, and was gone. Sanderson's jaw tightened. It had been one of Pablo Mendoza's men. The Mexican captain had caught up. He should have guessed the Rurale would be smart enough to estimate their destination, abandon the flat, and close in on a time-saving direct line.

He spun and swept the party with an appraising look. They were ready to move out.

"Got to get rid of Mendoza fast," he said in a low voice. "Virg, head up the mountain. Climb until you find a ledge that will take you north. And stay in the brush and trees much as you can."

The gunman nodded his understanding.

"I'll cut back," Frank continued; "try to draw them off."

Kate London stirred impatiently. "Won't we lose time that way? There's only three of them—four of us. Why do we have to run?"

"You don't kill a man unless you have to," Sanderson said coldly. "Move out," he finished, and he swung toward the waiting chestnut.

Kate's voice halted him. "I'm not saying we should, but we'd be protecting my property."

"Matter of opinion, who it belongs to."

"Why do you say that? It's mine more than anybody else's."

Exasperated by her stubbornness, Frank stood motionless for a few moments, then crossed to where his horse was tethered. He vaulted aboard and faced her. "Seems the Mexican government's taking a different view. That gold belonged to somebody before your husband got his hands on it." He motioned to Peck. "Keep it quiet."

The gunman nodded and struck off up the slope. The pack mules, no longer requiring lead ropes, filed in behind him. Kate, her face angry, followed them, and last of all came Billy Farr. When they were under way and climbing steadily, Sanderson wheeled about and, with the feeble rays of a cloud-shrouded sunrise in his eyes, angled toward the edge of the flat.

He wasted no energy trying to figure out what Mendoza had in mind; he knew only that he must turn the Rurales, suck them away from Calaveras Canyon—and do it without gunplay. Shooting would accomplish nothing more than to further alert the Apaches and betray their exact position.

Reaching the bottom of the slope, he broke through the fringe of brush and rode boldly into the open. He paused there, careful not to glance to his left, where he knew Mendoza to be. Instead, he turned his attention in the opposite direction. After a short delay, he raised himself in his stirrups. Now facing right, he made a forward gesture toward the south and spurred the chestnut into motion.

He dared not look back, but Pablo Mendoza, he hoped, had believed the brief pantomime—had thought that he was signaling to the remainder of the party, out of sight in the brush, and that all were now moving along the mountain, searching for the treasure.

Sanderson carried on the ruse until, a long mile later, he rounded a bulging shoulder of rock that blocked him from the rear. Instantly he wheeled into a narrow arroyo hard to his right and began to ascend the slope. Heeding his own instructions to Peck, he kept to the undergrowth. An hour later, as he was slicing diagonally across the grade, he caught sight of his party.

He did not know if the trick had worked, but he had seen no more evidence of the Rurales and felt certain that he had drawn them off. Mendoza and his men would have been maintaining a sharp watch on the mountain and could scarcely have afforded to ignore his actions, since they had no proof to the contrary.

It wouldn't end there, however. They would still have to be reckoned with later—but that was yet to come. It was best to take one thing at a time.

He rejoined the others, riding past Farr and Kate, aware of her cool silence, past the mules and up to where he was beside Peck. The gunman glanced at him, his brows lifted questioningly.

Sanderson said "I think it worked."

"See any Apaches?"

Frank shook his head and pointed to a rise some distance in front of them. "Figure to take a look when we get there. If they're around, we'll spot them from that point."

"You want to pull up, rest a bit?"

Sanderson said, "Keep moving. We'll stop on the rise."

He moved out ahead of the gunman. The animals were lathered from the steady climb under the now broiling sun, but it was only smart to get as far from Mendoza as possible—and do it fast. He glanced at the desert, now a vast, gleaming panorama of harsh colors. The clouds that had given promise of cooler weather at sunrise had drifted back onto the horizon and now lay there in a jumbled mass of dirty gray. There would be no relief.

He gained the rocky lip and, dismounting, made his way to the edge. From there he had a much broader view of the slope and the country below it, but his careful probing turned up nothing.

They rested on the high saddle for a half hour and then moved on. The grade steepened with the increasing heat, and shortly Sanderson directed all to dismount and walk. It was easier then, but much slower. Near noon they gained the first bench. There, however, they faced a sheer cliff, and they were forced to double back a quarter mile before they located a narrow gash, filled with loose, treacherous shale, that enabled them to climb its face and reach the wind-swept shelf.

Again they rested in the hot, sullen silence, then finally pushed on with Sanderson again in the lead. It was not a difficult passage; the bench was a good six feet in width and sloped inward. They made fair time. Near the middle of the afternoon, it began to drop, narrowing as it fused into the slope itself.

Progress, although down grade, slowed, as there was no distinct trail to follow and the hillside was steep, causing the horses to slip and slide several times. And then finally they were once more on level ground, crossing a small, flinty meadow that ended at the rim of a butte.

Frank Sanderson halted there and waited while the others ranged up beside him. He pointed to a narrow break in the mountain a quarter mile distant.

"That's it," he said. "That's Calaveras Canyon."

CHAPTER THIRTEEN

Kate London moved up beside Sanderson, her lips tight. Somewhere back on the steep hillside, a squirrel scolded the falling darkness.

"At last," she murmured. "At last." And then her tone hardened. "If we hadn't lost so much time climbing up the mountain—if we'd got here earlier—"

"Would've made no difference," Frank cut in. "Still had to wait for night. Heat—and the Indians."

"Going to be plenty light, anyway," Peck said.

"That'll work for us—and against us. Don't know which is best."

"But we are going in there—soon as it's dark?" Kate persisted.

Sanderson nodded. Billy Farr asked, "You know right where your husband hid the gold, Missus London?"

"Just about. Back in the canyon pretty far."

"That covers a lot of rough ground," Sanderson observed. "And we're going to be short on time."

"I think I know the exact spot—almost."

Peck groaned. Frank Sanderson shrugged. "Hope you do. Our heads are on the chopping block every minute we spend in there."

"Don't worry," Kate said. "I can find it."

There was a long silence. Finally Virg Peck asked, "You want to hole up here 'till sundown?"

"Good a place as any," Frank said, dismounting. He waited while the others came off their saddles. "Start practicing being quiet right now. Calaveras is a box canyon. Sound will carry a long way."

Peck rubbed at his whiskers. "Means we got to come back out the same way we go in. Bad if somebody slips in behind us."

Sanderson removed his spurs and hung them on the saddle horn. Squatting, his back to a rock, he said, "Heard there was a trail back in there somewhere. Never saw it myself. Probably be too steep for animals even if we were lucky enough to find it."

His eyes moved about the small area, touched the others taking their ease, and drifted on to the flat beyond the foot of the mountain where the shadows were lengthening. He wondered about Mendoza and his Rurales. They would have discovered their error by now; likely they were somewhere below, combing the brush.

And the outlaws—what had happened to them? There had been two separate clouds of dust. Where were they? Were they also on the slope, searching for the party they felt would lead them to the treasure? It was probable, and Frank Sanderson could only hope he and those with him could get into the canyon, recover the gold, and depart before their exit was blocked.

He had seen no more Indian sign, but there was no comfort in that thought. They were deep in Apache country and perhaps were being watched by the copper-skinned warriors at that very moment. He wondered how the Indians would react. Would they attack the instant they saw whites moving into the canyon, or would they hold off until they were sure these were the persons they wanted? He stirred restlessly. You could never figure an Apache. It was useless to try.

He paused, listening to the small talk passing between Kate and the boy.

"Are you married, Billy?" she asked.

"No, ma'am. Got me a girl, though. Meg, her name is. Soon as I'm paid off, I aim to marry up with her. Been knocking around for almost a year now, trying to find myself a decent job so's we could get hitched. Just never had the luck."

"Where is she now?"

"Little burg name of Mesilla—north of El Paso."

"I know where it is."

"She's waiting there for me to come get her. Been promising I'd do that—come riding up with my pockets full of gold eagles—all fixed to buy us a nice place where we can have a home and a family."

"Have you a place already picked out?"

"Yes'm. Down in Mexico. Don't take much money there—American money, I mean. Always figured I'd like to go there, set myself up with a ranch."

Sanderson studied Farr through half-closed lids. Envy stirred vaguely through him. A young man with big plans. Everything ahead of him. If they made it back with Kate London's treasure, all of Billy Farr's dreams would come true. He would have his wife, his ranch—and live the way he wished.

What can I look forward to?

He considered the question bitterly. Aimless wandering. Empty trails. Saloons. Flea-bit hotels. Sure, he would have cash in his pockets—fifteen hundred good, round dollars, which was a hell of a lot of money when you thought about it. But it wouldn't buy whatever it was he needed to soothe his soul.

If he was smart, he'd get himself a piece of land, the way the boy intended to do. That way he'd be buying into something permanent. But Frank Sanderson knew himself well enough to recognize the fallacy of that idea. He could never be a rancher. Nursing a bunch of cows and red-eyed steers was not for him. He'd lived too long with danger and excitement to ever stay put with a deal like that.

Go back to Kansas Bend?

That had occurred to him before when he was at odds with himself. Always he had brushed aside the idea. But he supposed he could return, let them pin a badge on him again…

Only he never would. He'd always be remembering how the people there had let him down, how they had demonstrated their lack of faith in him. He'd be forever wondering about the next time when something arose to cast doubts as to his honesty or ability. No, he wanted none of it—none of the law…

The law. He had tried to make it mean something in Kansas Bend—justice and square dealing and absolute honesty. He had believed in it himself, fought often and hard to make others respect it. Then suddenly he had found himself on the opposite end of the fence—and the law he had championed had been his enemy.

Sanderson stirred restlessly. It must have caused a lot of deep belly laughs among the renegades and card sharps and other shadowy characters he had come up against when they got the news; probably did them a lot of good to see him slapped down by the selfsame law he had always declared infallible.

Drifters had the right idea. Just rock along, pick up a stake whenever you had the need for one. Never fret about anything. Just ride—and keep riding, like a cottonwood leaf caught up by the wind. Maybe it wasn't the complete life, but it had no complications.

Again Kate London's voice touched him. "When you set the day for your wedding, Billy, let me know. I'd like to do something for you and your bride. A nice gift, maybe. Something to help you get your ranch started."

"Be real fine, Missus London, real fine. You tell me where you'll be and I'll see you get the word."

Kate was a woman beneath that cold crust, Frank thought, getting to his feet. And soft-hearted, too. She'd probably hand over an extra thousand or so to the boy before it was done with. Guilt was squirming around inside her like a panful of maggots, and she was trying to buy off her conscience by being generous with someone else.

Well, it meant nothing to him. It was her gold—if they got it—and she could give it all away if she liked, as long as she paid off Virg Peck and him.

He made a swift, sweeping survey of the skyline. The sun's afterglow had vanished; stars were breaking out like small lanterns suddenly lighted. It would be bright, as Peck had noted, once the moon swung into position. He lowered his eyes to the others.

"Let's go," he said. "Lead your horses. If you have to talk—whisper."

"How about the mules?" Peck asked.

"We'll each take one—you, Billy, and I," he replied, crossing to where the chestnut stood. Taking the rope of the nearest pack animal, he secured it to his saddle.

After a moment the gunman said, "All set."

Sanderson led off, picking a trail as best he could. He sought the natural aisles between trees and undergrowth, carefully avoiding the rock-studded patches of open ground whenever possible. To him, as they worked slowly toward the mouth of the canyon, they seemed to be creating an abnormal amount of noise, but he knew he could expect no better; it was not possible for four persons and the animals to move without causing some racket.

They reached the absolute bottom of the grade and came out alongside a massive pile of boulders and crumbling shale. Storm-loosened, it had at some time in the past come roaring down from the mountain's higher levels to form a shoulder at the southern end of the canyon's mouth. Frank started a slow circuit of the formation, then abruptly halted, lifting his hand in warning.

Stepping away from the gelding, he cocked an ear toward the flat, now less than a hundred yards distant. He could not see the near edge, as the dense brush and mounds of rock screened it from him.

"What is it?" Kate asked in a tense voice.

He waved her to stillness. He had heard—or thought he did—the click of metal against stone. It had come from nearby—just beyond the fringe of growth. He turned to Kate and the others, his face highlighted by the growing star-shine.

"Wait," he murmured.

Ground-reining the chestnut, be bent low and faded into the shadows. It would not have been an Apache; they rode unshod horses, and the iron shoes of the animals they stole from ranchers and the Army were always quickly removed to be hammered into knives, arrowheads, spear points and similar needed items. It could be Mendoza—possibly even the outlaws he had been expecting to turn up...

Again there was sound. He halted. A rider moved into view. The man was turned from him, looking to the south. In moments he was joined by two more, and all walked their mounts into the open. There was no mistaking them in the light: Mendoza and his Rurales.

Sanderson waited. A coyote chorus far back on the slope began to fill the night with weird, discordant music. A dove mourned in loneliness. Mendoza and his men were soft blurs, completely motionless. Suddenly they came about, and following a trail along the fringe of underbrush, they struck north. Sanderson's shoulders went down in relief. They were moving away from the canyon.

He remained quiet, watching the soldiers pass beyond his field of vision; stalled out another minute to be sure they were beyond the entrance of Calaveras; then, wheeling, he hurried back to his party.

"Mendoza," he said, picking up the chestnut's leathers. "Heading away from us."

"Figured it was time he showed up," Peck said.

Frank nodded. "Knows we're around close— and he'll keep hunting until he finds us. Got to move fast—get the gold and move out. With a little luck we can do it."

"With a little luck," Virg Peck said, "and no Apaches jumping us."

CHAPTER FOURTEEN

They circled the shoulder, keeping behind the irregular wall of brush and rock. Then, angling left, they followed the foot of the mountain for a short distance. At last, when the mouth of the canyon yawned blackly before them, they turned and began a slow climb.

The entrance was narrow, no more than fifty yards across. It was choked with brush, and there was no distinct trail. Sanderson, still leading, again picked a route around the boulders and between the tough, stubby growth, seeking, as before, to make their passage quiet and yet not too difficult for the horses and mules.

Immediately they became aware of the heat that lay trapped in the restricted confines of the canyon. Absorbed and stored by huge, flat slabs of granite and sandstone during the long swing of the sun across the heavens, it was just then beginning to dissipate. Sudden, dry reports, like small gunshots, continually startled them.

The brush was powder-dry. A combination of no rain and the searing heat, day after day, had turned the canyon into a tinder box. Noting this, Frank Sanderson realized that if the Apaches wanted them badly enough they had but to set fires at the canyon's mouth. Flames would roar upwind with terrible speed, trapping them completely, unless the old trail at the far end could be found.

He doubted if the Apaches would want it that way; more than likely they would lie in hiding, bide their time until they were certain these were the whites responsible for the deaths of their tribesmen. Convinced, they would then move in and capture, rather than kill immediately. Revenge was a way of life with the dark-faced warriors, and they would look forward to the sport of torture before they permitted death to remove their captives.

They pushed on, boring deeper into the dust-laden channel between high, steep walls. The horses were nervous, did not like the place at all. The whites of their eyes showed, and they continually tossed their heads, seeking to jerk free, which set up a constant ringing of harness metal. Picketing must be secure, or they would break and run.

Halfway up the canyon, a rock ledge barred their way. Sanderson turned aside and halted in a small swale surrounded by scrub oak, mahogany, and stunted pine. It would be as good a place as any from which to base the search—and it afforded effective cover for the animals.

Sanderson tied the chestnut to a stout bush and cautioned the others. "Put a hard knot in your lead ropes. Horses are spooky. Don't want them pulling loose."

"We leave the mules here too?" Peck asked.

"Yes," Sanderson said, in a low whisper. "Chests will be heavy—awkward to handle.

We'll carry in saddlebags."

They moved about slowly in the hush, making their preparations. Sanderson crossed to where Kate had tethered her sorrel and inspected the rope. Satisfied, he checked the other horses as well as the mules. All were tightly anchored. He turned then to Kate.

"Up to you from here on."

She stepped to the center of the bowl and gazed at the walls thrusting upward from either side. Moonlight was now showering down strongly, augmenting the starshine, and the world around them was all silver and shadow.

"Dan said there was a butte—a sort of cliff formation. Near the end of the canyon."

"Which side?"

She shook her head. "He didn't say—and I never thought to ask. I got the idea, somehow, that it was on the left." Kate paused and looked at Sanderson. She was pale, her face taut.

"I—I didn't think it would be like this—so wild, so forbidding. Like a graveyard."

"It's the stillness," Frank said, hoping to calm her.

He stared into the depths of the canyon. A butte—Dan London had told his wife. He thought back, tried to recall his early visit into the area. There had been several such formations. Placing this particular one near the end of the slash narrowed it down some—but it could be on either side. It could take hours to locate.

He saw his hope of getting the chore done

quickly begin to fade.

Somewhere on the slope, a displaced bit of gravel clattered hollowly down grade. The sound, exaggerated by the silence, brought them up sharp. One of the horses tugged anxiously at his rope. Sanderson felt tension mount within him: Animal or Apache? He waited, a tall, half-bent shape etched against his surroundings. Only the slow, ragged breathing of Billy Farr broke the hush. An owl hooted. The lawman's eyes narrowed. He continued to wait. A soft chirping came from farther along.

Sanderson straightened slowly, giving no outward evidence of being disturbed. The Indians were there—he knew that now. Likely they were scattered along the canyon's rim. He wondered again what their plan would be—attack or delay until they were sure they were getting the man they wanted? And in either event, would they hold off until sunrise? It was a mistake to think they would not fight at night; Apaches followed whichever course best suited their needs and purposes.

He turned to Kate London. "Last chance to change your mind," he murmured.

She shook her head. "I've come this far—I won't quit now."

"Let's go," he said then. "String out in a line, across the canyon. Keep a sharp watch for that butte." He paused and again faced Kate. "Anything special about the one we want?"

"No—only that it's not high."

They separated, Sanderson and Peck taking up positions at the extreme ends, Kate and Farr in the center. The bottom of the canyon was not wide, no more than two dozen yards at that particular point, so there was little danger of anyone's getting lost from the others.

They worked up the canyon gradually, with the heat becoming more noticeable as they moved deeper into the slash. The temperature would hold until midnight or so before it would lower. By early morning a chill would settle over the rugged depths, only to die quickly with the rising of the sun, after which the process would begin all over again.

Progress was slow, tedious. Briarbush tore at their legs, impeded their passage. Huge boulders barred their way, forcing them to climb around or over weather-smoothed surfaces. Sanderson, relying on Kate to spot the butte, kept his own eyes probing the slopes and ridges.

Unexpectedly, an oath blurted from Billy Farr's lips. He leaped to one side as a rabbit skittered from beneath his feet and went dodging from side to side into the clumps of snakeweed and saltbush. The boy's pistol had come up with amazing speed. Sanderson breathed a sigh for the good fortune that had stayed Billy's trigger finger. Had he fired, everyone within miles would know of their position.

At that moment he saw—or thought he saw—motion on the rim above.

It was no more than a brief glimpse, a low

silhouette that broke the skyline for only an instant. Frank felt his pulse quicken as all the old deep-seated signals of alarm rushed to the surface. Speculation had come to an end: The Apaches were there. He wondered how many. He glanced along the line. No one else had seen the fleeting movement. It was just as well. Subconsciously he reached down, touched the pistol at his hip, and reassured himself.

They moved on, endeavoring to walk quietly, ignoring the discomfort of sweat, the rough footing beneath him, the clawing underbrush. Sanderson's eyes continued to rake the rim and the slopes. One Apache would mean more....

"There it is—the bluff! I'm sure of it!"

Kate's low, husky cry caught at him, bringing him around. He hurried to her.

"It's exactly as Dan described it!"

He followed her leveled finger. It could be the one—a long-running bluff, scarcely six feet in height at the most. They were not far from the end of the canyon.

The memory of the dark silhouette still in his mind, Sanderson said, "Virg, you and Billy keep walking. Kate and I will have a look."

"Why don't we all take a look?" Farr demanded, his voice rising slightly.

"A good reason. If the Apaches are watching, it'll be smart to act like we haven't found the gold. Figure that's what's holding them back: They're not sure we're the ones they're laying for."

"Funny we ain't seen nothing, or heard nothing" Virgil Peck said. "Was guessing they'd be down on us before now."

"They're out there—but they're holding off for some reason."

"Could be there's only a couple—sort of like sentries, keeping an eye on the place. They've spotted us, and now they're high-tailing it after the rest of the tribe so's everybody can get in on the kill."

Kate shuddered. Sanderson said, "Could be, but let's play it smart. Keep walking, like I told you. When you get to the end of the canyon, double back. Meet you here."

The gunman was staring off into the dark brush.

"Was we smart, we'd get the hell out of here—quick."

"Never!" Kate London said. "Not now!"

Frank grinned tightly at the firmness in her voice. Neither hell nor hallelujah would stop Kate London now.

"She's right," he said. "Be fools to back off now. Move on."

Peck did not stir. Sanderson looked at him sharply. "Something wrong?"

Virgil's face was a stiff mask. His eyes seemed to have receded; they were now small, shadowed pockets. "Nothing's wrong," he murmured, and he started forward.

Sanderson wheeled toward Kate, and together they headed into the brush. He did not look back to see if Peck and Billy Farr had continued—he simply assumed they had—but a deep worry was dragging at him as he thought of Peck's actions. He had just looked upon naked fear.

Every man knew fear in his heart; Frank Sanderson had come to that conclusion years before. It was a natural facet of a man's nature, a part of living, doing. But it did not ordinarily freeze his brain, paralyze his muscles into immobility, and turn him aside. It served instead to sharpen his abilities, flood him with a determination to survive, win out. Somehow it did not seem possible that Virgil Peck could be an absolute coward—even if Apaches were involved.

They gained the base of the butte, breathing heavily from the short but steep climb. Sanderson went first. He reached back for Kate's hand and drew her onto the shelf that fronted the formation.

"Near—the center—" she gasped, her body heaving.

He clawed his way to the middle of the cliff. Off to his right he could hear the sounds of Peck and Farr moving up the canyon and he derived some relief from that.

A mound of dead branches, leaves, and gravel laid a barrier ahead of him in the ledge. He paused for a moment, considering the obstacle. Then, not attempting to push aside the accumulation of wind-blown debris, he crawled behind it.

Abruptly be halted. Elation swept through him. The dark, oblong shapes of three iron-bound chests were before him. He scrambled forward, his hand groping for the hasp of the nearest. He jerked it open and raised the lid of the dust-covered box. It was filled to level with dully glinting coins.

"Kate—it's here!" he called in a hoarse voice.

"Thank God!" he heard her say fervently. "Oh—thank God!"

CHAPTER FIFTEEN

Sanderson drew himself to one side, making room for Kate London. She was breathing in short, tortured gasps, and he could feel the trembling of her body.

"The others—are they full too?"

He unsnapped the rusting hasps of the two remaining chests and raised their dome-shaped lids. Gold filled each. He gathered up a handful of the coins, passed some to her and fell to examining the rest.

"Mexican gold pieces," he said.

She looked at him, instantly worried. "Aren't they any good?"

"Sure. Worth ten, maybe twelve dollars American, at least. Not old stuff."

"You mean the coins are the kind they use

now?"

He nodded. "All probably belonged to some bank, or even the government, and was taken in a holdup."

"Then the smugglers tried to get it out of the country."

Kate returned the coins to him; he dumped the lot back into the chest and closed the lid.

"That's why the Rurales have been following us," she said. "They heard about Dan hiding it—and now they're going to try and get it back."

"About the size of it."

"But I didn't steal it from whoever owned it. It was someone else—the smugglers, perhaps. Then the Apaches had it—and finally my husband. Actually, he found it. I think I've as much right to it as anybody."

Sanderson shrugged at her logic. "Not arguing with you, one way or the other. I'm just the hired help." He pulled back and glanced into the canyon. "Peck and the boy ought to be showing up. Quick as they're here, we'll load up the saddlebags and move on."

Kate, flat on her back, gazing up into the starry canopy bending overhead, sighed contentedly. She seemed to have forgotten the possibility of their never leaving the canyon.

"Frank—how much is there? In American money, I mean?"

He studied her quietly. In the pale light her features were soft-edged, and her eyes appeared wide and deep. Kate London could be beautiful, he realized, when she permitted herself to be so. In times past she likely had made many a man's heart skip a beat.

"How much?" she asked again.

He caught himself and stirred. "Twenty, maybe thirty thousand dollars. Hard to tell—but there's enough to last you a long time." He swung his attention once more to the brush. There was a dry rustling off near the center. "That'll be Virg and Billy," he said, and he reached for the saddlebags he had hung across a low bush. "Start filling this. I'll get the others."

The chests loaded the four pairs of bags comfortably. When they had finished and were again on the floor of the hushed canyon, Sanderson plucked at Peck's arm.

"Any Apache sign farther up?"

The gunman shook his head. "Didn't see nothing—but I got a bad feeling. It's been too easy."

"Long way from being out of here yet," Frank said.

"Just what I mean. Apaches are just teasing us along."

Billy Farr rubbed his hands together vigorously. "Shucks, I don't think there's any Indians around here. We'd a heard from them before now. They're doing their looking in the daytime."

"Nobody comes in here while the sun's up," Sanderson said, irritated by the boy's tone.

97

"Heat gets over a hundred—place is like a furnace. Everybody ready?"

They started off into the silence of the night. Sanderson glanced back. Kate's features were calm, almost pleased, as though there were nothing more to fear. Virg Peck still wore the same drawn mask. Billy Farr was smiling, a light, oily shine on his cheeks. Likely he was already dreaming about his girl, Meg, and the ranch they would soon have. He wished he too could dismiss the hours that lay ahead so easily.

They pressed on, facing a cooling wind that came in from the desert. Sanderson kept his eyes roving the slopes and the rim above. He saw nothing except the dark, ragged shape of rocks, deep shadows, gaunt cholla cactus, and stunted trees. Angry exasperation shook him. If the Apaches were there—why didn't they make their move? It was worse not knowing—almost.

He quickened the pace, anxious now to reach the horses and get out of the canyon. Maybe they were going to be lucky. Maybe he had been wrong about the Indians. But it was best not to press it. The thing to do was get out of Calaveras Canyon as soon as possible.

As tension pressed with greater intensity upon him, it seemed the distance from the butte to the camp had trebled, but finally they came in sight of the picketed animals. Slinging the bags across the mules' rigging, they gathered in the center of the clearing. To the east the first haze of a new day was just beginning to show.

"We taking time to eat a bite?" Billy Farr asked. "Sure am hungry."

"Later," Sanderson snapped. "We'd be fools to hang around here any longer than necessary."

The boy shrugged. "Still figure you're loco. No Indians watching us. We'd a seen them by now."

"You go right on thinking that," Frank said, as he began to free his horse. "Rest of us are moving on fast as we can.

"Same as before," he said quietly as they all lined up. He was fighting an almost uncontrollable urge to get them all into the saddle and make a dash for the flats beyond the canyon. "Virg—lead off. Then Kate and Farr, and the mules. I'll bring up the rear."

He was struggling to keep his voice even, not to betray the anxiety that gripped him. This was the final test—the long, slow trip out. Facing Mendoza and several outlaws would be nothing—if they could get by the Apaches.

He watched Peck head out, leading his black. Kate fell in behind the gunman as directed, and then Billy and the mules. They strung out across the open ground, moving quietly but all, unconsciously, moved to haste.

The sharp, spiteful crack of a rifle suddenly shattered the stillness, sending a bounding barrage of echoes along the canyon walls. One of the mules plunged head first to the ground.

"Down!"

Frank Sanderson yelled the warning as he wheeled, wrenched his rifle from its boot, and rushing Kate ahead of him, ducked into the brush.

CHAPTER SIXTEEN

More rifle shots ripped through the night. Dust spurted upward in small, quick geysers as bullets plowed into the bone-dry soil. Smoke began to drift lazily up the canyon. Caught in the vicious firing, the horses milled about in the center of the clearing.

Crouched behind a boulder, Frank Sanderson tried to locate the rest of his party. Kate London had pulled back under a low, brush-covered overhang. He didn't think the Apaches could see her. She was safe—at least for the time being.

A dozen paces to his left, Virgil Peck was crouched behind a rotted stump. Using his pistol, he was firing steadily at the Indians scattered along the slope. Virg had been right, apparently: The main party of Apaches had not been in the canyon—had come when summoned by a sentinel.

It would have been wise to pull out when Peck had suggested it—only they would have failed their promise to Kate in recovering the treasure. Sanderson's mouth pulled into a wry grin; gold wasn't worth much to them now.

Looking over his shoulder, he endeavored to spot Billy Farr. He saw the boy, hunched low on hands and knees, leading the two remaining pack mules into the brush on the opposite side of the clearing.

Relieved, Sanderson turned back to the slope. No one had been hit; the mule had been the only casualty. It was something of a miracle, he thought, levering his rifle and targeting the tell-tale puffs of smoke below the rim.

He triggered steadily, but it was impossible to determine whether he scored or not. He did note, with satisfaction, that shots no longer came from several points. Either his bullets had found their mark or the Apache hidden there had changed his position.

The rifle clicked on an empty chamber. Rolling to his back, he dug into his pockets for additional cartridges, but found only a few. There was a full box on his saddle, but they were of no use to him now. Cursing himself for such carelessness, be reloaded. Half a magazine. Like Peck, he'd be depending upon his pistol very soon.

The weapon again ready, Sanderson crawled deeper into the brush and worked his way nearer to Kate London. Her face, when she turned toward him, had lost its color, and her eyes were wide—dazed.

"Use that gun you're wearing!" be shouted.

The harshness of his tone seemed to jar her

from the lethargy that gripped her. She nodded woodenly, drew the pistol, and began to fire it in the general direction of the slope.

"Aim!" Sanderson yelled in exasperation. "Point at the smoke! "

Peck, hearing, paused. He turned to Frank, stared briefly, spat, and then resumed his firing.

A spatter of bullets laced the ground in front of the lawman, showering him with dirt. He jerked back, brushing at his eyes, swearing angrily. Another fool move like that and he'd be the second casualty.

There was a sudden hammer of hoofs. He looked up. The last burst of shooting had been too much for the horses. They surged toward the far side of the open area, leaped a low roll of scrub oak, and disappeared. A moment later, Sanderson saw the head of his chestnut bob into view. The gelding had run a few yards and halted and was now waiting uncertainly.

There was no sign of Billy Farr and the mules. That the younger man had succeeded in getting the pack animals out of the clearing was evident, but there were no shots coming from that point. Farr could have paid with his life for his efforts.

Carefully, Sanderson began to worm his way down the slope until he was halfway between Kate London and Peck.

"They got Billy—I think!" he shouted, opening up.

The gunman turned to him again. His eyes

were dull and flat, his mouth a thin line. "Matter of time for all of us," he said, adding, "The goddam murdering gut-eaters!"

"Not rushing us," Frank yelled back. "Could mean they're not sure. Might have a chance yet to get to the horses."

Peck shook his head. "Fooling yourself. It's the way they work. Part of them'll keep us pinned down; rest will sneak in through the brush."

There was a note of desperation in the gunman's voice, and suddenly he was firing erratically, almost blindly.

"Maybe. But they won't move straight into our fire. How's your ammunition holding out?"

Sanderson's words seemed to steady Peck somewhat. He paused and glanced down. "Couple dozen rounds."

"Start picking your shots. First lull we get, work toward those rocks to your right. Horses are on the other side of the clearing—back of us."

He turned to repeat the instructions to Kate. She was on her knees, hunkered low, making good use of the pistol. She held the heavy weapon with both hands, and each time she pressed the trigger, it bucked wildly. She listened to him impassively, nodding her understanding.

Almost at once the shooting on the slope began to taper off, then to dwindle to a thin spatter. It was as if the Apaches were reminding them that they were still trapped and that there was no escape.

"Hell's coming now," Peck said, glancing over his shoulder. "Wish them damn horses was closer. Could make a run for them."

"Got to circle around through the brush first," the lawman said. "We'd not cover ten steps in the open."

"Better than letting them grab us," Peck replied in an odd voice. "You don't know what them devils can do to a man, once they set their minds to it. Or a woman."

Grim, Sanderson probed the hillside before him, trying to see through the pall of smoke. A dark shape, low to the ground, moved across a narrow aisle separating two rocks. He took quick aim and pressed off a bullet. The shadowy blur sank lower and remained still.

He wondered how many Apaches were still hiding on the slope. Fewer than a dozen, he guessed. He and Virg Peck had greatly cut down the odds. If only Harvey Neff—or Farr—were there to help, matters might turn out right. He looked again to where he had last seen the boy. Billy was dead; there could be no other explanation for his silence.

"Start circling towards the horses," he said, becoming abruptly aware that the shooting was at its lowest point. "Doubt if we'll get a better chance. I'll see to Kate."

Peck nodded and started to pull back. "Was they a might closer—"

A loud burst of yells broke through the gunman's words. Sanderson spun and saw the dark shape of an Indian lunge at Virg. He fired quickly. The Apache jolted and fell to one side. More appeared, coming in on Peck's right, screaming as they leaped over rocks and through the brush.

Frank saw others moving in at his left. He dropped to one knee and turned his gun on them. The rifle was empty. He threw it aside, dragged out his revolver, and downed a shrieking brave who was almost upon him. Peck was not shooting. Frank wheeled toward him.

Virg was upright, a deep frown on his face. He seemed frozen, unable to function. His pistol hung limply from his fingers. Beyond him an Apache, knife drawn, was rushing in.

"Look out!" Sanderson yelled, and he drove a bullet into the Indian.

Solid force hit him from behind and carried him forward. He felt sweaty arms go about his head and neck. Instantly he dropped flat and jerked free. Still prone, he fired at close quarters into the Apache beside him; then he bounded to his feet.

A fresh eruption of gunfire lifted from the lower end of the clearing. Hope surged through Sanderson. Billy Farr! The boy wasn't dead! Then, from the corner of his eye, he saw three riders wheel into view and he knew he was wrong. Pablo Mendoza and his men.

Apaches seemed to be everywhere. He threw

a glance toward Kate. Crouched behind an oak clump, she was still firing. A bullet plucked at Sanderson's sleeve. He wheeled instinctively. The paint-smeared face of a brave, mouth open in a wild yell, was before him. He triggered the pistol twice in rapid succession. The face dissolved in a splatter of blood.

Another piercing scream brought Sanderson back around. Peck was lunging toward him, his face working convulsively.

"Horse!" the gunman yelled. "Get—my—horse!"

Frank grabbed for the gunman's arm. "No—wait! We got some help—the Rurales—"

Virg Peck wrenched free. He stumbled, recovered himself, staggered on, and reached the center of the clearing.

"My horse—"

Half a dozen guns raked the open ground. Peck hesitated, then spun slowly. He sank to his knees, lips still mouthing soundless words, and then abruptly sprawled full length.

CHAPTER SEVENTEEN

The Apaches had shifted their attack to the lower end of the canyon, concentrating now on Mendoza and his men. Sanderson could see the Mexicans wheeling in and out of the brush and rocks, their horses lathered and wild-eyed, having a hard time of it.

He seized the moment to dash into the open, grasp Peck by the arms, and drag him into the sheltering brush. The gunman was barely alive. He stared at Frank through glazing eyes.

"Get...out of...here," he mumbled. "Don't let them...get you...or...the woman...."

A spasm of pain tore at his features. He twisted to one side, then went limp. Seething anger rocked Sanderson. Peck dead. And Neff and Billy Farr. Kate London and he would be next—all for three chests of gold—gold none of them would ever see again.

Grim, he looked up. The clearing was unnaturally quiet under the drifting layers of smoke. Maybe it wasn't all over for Kate and him yet.

He jerked about and glanced toward the mouth of the canyon. Mendoza wheeled into view, only the upper portion of his body visible. The Rurale officer, a pistol in each hand, was firing coolly as he weaved in and out of the brush. One of his men was nearby. There was no sign of the third.

Sanderson's hopes sank. That route of escape was blocked. Abruptly he came to his feet. *Up the canyon*—that was the answer! While the Apaches were busy with the Mexicans, he and Kate could make a run for it. They might find a place to hide—could possibly locate the trail he had heard about. Take the horses—they would make better time, at least for a while, and if they were lucky enough to find the trail—

He wheeled and again looked toward the lower end of the canyon. He could see only Mendoza now. He was farther away, fighting to reach the flat. His two men were not to be seen; either they had made it or both were dead. Regardless, the Indians would soon turn and come racing back to complete the job they had begun in the clearing. Ducking low, he hurried to Kate, pausing only long enough to snatch up his empty rifle.

"We've got one chance—up the canyon," he said, reaching for her hand. "Have to move fast. Apaches will be coming."

She nodded and, taking his fingers in hers, followed him into the brush. They circled the open ground at a run, not daring to show themselves. There could be an Indian or two still on the slope, besides the possibility of being seen from below.

They reached the opposite side and halted. Frank peered anxiously into the welter of scrubby undergrowth, now lightening with the advancing dawn. He located the chestnut, standing in an oak thicket. Nearby was Virg Peck's black. The remaining horses were not to be seen; apparently they had continued to run once they had broken out of the trap.

"No time to hunt your horse," he said, hurrying to the gelding. "Ride the black."

They reached the two mounts. Sanderson boosted Kate into the saddle, then glanced critically at her booted foot in the stirrup. Luckily, she was about the same height as the gunman. She would be able to manage until they were a safe distance away; then he could take time to shorten the leather.

Jamming his rifle into the boot, he swung up. It was still quiet in the clearing. They were getting a good start.

"Sanderson—"

He turned to Kate.

"What about the gold?"

He stared at her. "Gold! Dead men laying around everywhere, Apaches breathing down our necks—and you think about that damned gold!"

"It's what we came for," she said coolly. "If we don't save it, everything that's happened has been for nothing. Even one saddlebag full—"

He threw her a furious look and spun the chestnut about savagely. Raising himself in the stirrups, he gazed down into the maze of brush where he had last seen Billy Farr. He could spot none of the mules.

Impatient, aware of the danger, he rode the gelding deeper into the undergrowth, head swinging back and forth as he searched for the boy's body. There was no sign of that either. Frowning, he dropped from the saddle and began to examine the ground. He had the correct location; he saw the small, neat imprints of the mules' shoes. Close by were deep scuff marks, made no doubt by the toes of Farr's boots.

With the knowledge that the Apaches could

be only a breath away hammering at him, he rose and studied the ground before him. The prints continued, striking off across the slope of the canyon. Suddenly he came to a halt—then rushed forward and knelt again. The full, perfect imprint of a man's boot heel slightly to the side of the hoof marks brought an oath to his lips.

The pack mules had been led off! Billy Farr was not dead at all! Somehow, during the first furious moments of the Apache attack, he had managed to slip through and reach the flats. And he had taken the gold with him—even that in the saddlebags that had been on the dead mule.

Sanderson delayed no further. Vaulting onto the chestnut, he returned to Kate.

"There's no gold," he said before she could voice a question. "Farr's gone—and took it with him."

"Gone!" she echoed blankly. "I thought they'd killed him. How could—"

"Got out before the Indians blocked the canyon. They were so damned busy with us they didn't see him."

A yell sounded in the clearing. The Apaches were back. Sanderson shouldered the gelding roughly against Kate's horse and got him turned around. Reaching down, he slapped the black smartly on the rump.

"Got to get out of here," he said in a low voice as the horse leaped away.

110

He swung in behind her, now and then glancing over his shoulder. After the first hundred yards both mounts began to slow because of the steep grade, then dropped to a walk. Kate's voice reached Sanderson.

"Where would Billy go?"

"Across the flats. If we make it out of this canyon, we'll be doing the same. Maybe we can pick up his tracks."

The horses plodded on, gradually working up the face of the slope. Twice they came to blank rock walls and were compelled to double back and take a different course. A mile passed. Sanderson, feeling the chestnut heaving under him, realized their mounts could go no farther carrying a load. He dismounted and called to Kate to do the same.

They had a fair lead, considering the rough country, and it should increase. They could count on the Apaches' losing time searching the rocks and brush for their trail. There was no more shooting. Everything was all over at the mouth of the canyon, he guessed.

The climb became more difficult. Hard rains at some time in the past had carved huge chunks from the side of the hill, leaving deep gashes across which the horses stumbled and slid and sometimes fell. Each time Frank feared one or both would break their legs, but somehow they came through, dust-plastered but unhurt.

He had seen nothing of the trail. At the be-

111

ginning they had simply angled upward, following the occasional paths created by weather and given further distinction by deer and other animals passing that way. The real trail, the lawman realized, could be on the north side.

That thought disturbed him. He had chosen the southern slope because it appeared less steep. If he were wrong, they should cross over as soon as possible, attempt to get high before the Apaches caught up.

On fairly high ground now, he began to study the opposite hillside, searching for the route that would lift them out of the slash and lead to the ridges and grassy saddles beyond.

The sun had finally broken over the eastern rim, dispelling the last of the shadows and charging the dry air with slowly rising heat. Soon the unbearable hours would come, increasing their problems. The horses were already beginning to lather.

On a level bench nearly three-quarters of the way to the crest, Sanderson called a halt. Both the chestnut and the black could go no farther without rest. Kate was in little better condition, and his own body ached from the unaccustomed exertion of climbing.

Kate settled gratefully on a rock and wiped at her face with the back of a hand. "There's been no more shooting," she said, looking off toward the mouth of the canyon. "I guess that means those men—the Mexicans—are dead too."

Frank nodded. "Last I saw of them, they were

trying to reach the flat. Doubt if they made it."

She sighed heavily. "So many dead. And nothing to show for it."

He looked at her closely. At last she was beginning to realize the price she had been so willing to pay when it had all begun. A curt reminder of that fact sprang to his lips. He let it pass. Kate London would have her conscience to reckon with; leave it at that.

He said, "I'm going to have a look around. Keep a watch on that slope below. Apaches will have found our tracks by now."

She nodded, and he moved ahead a short distance. Swinging his glance in a slow circle, he again checked the opposite hillside. Nothing. He shifted his eyes to the end of the canyon, now visible. Again nothing. He came on around to the slope lifting above them. His attention came to a halt. A startled oath broke from his lips. Kate got to her feet.

"What is it?"

"That trail—that goddam trail—it's above us! We've been traveling underneath it!"

She hurried toward him, her eyes lighting. She followed his leveled finger. "I see it! Between those two big rocks."

"That's it. We missed it below somewhere— probably at the last butte. Wasn't enough light to see good." He paused and considered the ledge soberly. "Not much help now. We can't go back. Bound to run head on into the Apaches."

"Maybe we can find a place along here. Or farther on."

"We've got to," the lawman said. "Else we—"

His words were lost in a sudden explosion of rock splinters and dust as a bullet smashed into the wall behind him.

CHAPTER EIGHTEEN

Sanderson lunged at Kate, caught her in his arms, and carried her to the ground. More bullets splattered against the rocks; others shrieked off into space. Drawing his pistol, Frank raised his head and peered down into the canyon. Two Apaches, dodging in and out of the brush, were moving up the slope. There would be others beyond them, scattered about.

"Got to get away from here—quick," he said.

He turned to the trail. Ten yards farther on was a bulging shoulder of rock. If they could reach it, they would have it standing between them and the Apaches' bullets. He touched Kate's shoulder and pointed to the massive outcrop of granite.

"When I open up, take the horses and lead them around that rock. Soon as you've made it, I'll follow."

She nodded. There was a smudge on the side of her face, a result of contact with the soil when he had borne her down. She brushed at it

114

and prepared to rise.

"I'm ready," she said.

Sanderson checked the cylinder of his pistol, assuring himself it was full. He was wishing he had the rifle, but it was on his saddle, beyond reach—and still empty. He gave her a brief nod and got to his knees.

"Now!" he said, and wheeling, he began to shoot at the figures working their way up the hillside.

One of the Indians threw his arms wide and fell over backward. Sanderson concentrated on the other. Behind him he could hear Kate scrambling over the rocks as she struggled with the reluctant horses. The second Apache, running frantically, plunged behind a mound of earth and stones. Sanderson pinned him down with a regularly spaced flow of bullets.

He glanced to Kate. She had reached the turn in the trail. The horses were pulling back, necks outstretched as they followed stubbornly. Finally, they rounded the shoulder and were out of sight.

Sanderson brought his attention back to the hiding Apache. Aiming at the point where he had last seen the man, he squeezed off a shot; then he leaped to his feet and raced to overtake Kate.

"Keep going!" he shouted when he gained the rock. "They'll be moving up."

He reloaded the pistol as he closed in beside Kate London. Then, relieving her of the chestnut's reins, he dropped back, permitting her to move on with her horse. The path was becoming steeper, and that set up a worry inside him. Unless they reached a defile soon where they could climb to the trail above, they would eventually come to a dead end.

Yells were lifting from the canyon. The remaining renegades had caught up with the scouts; now all would come swarming up the slope. He wheeled toward the gelding and pulled the rifle from its scabbard. Digging into a saddle pocket, he procured the box of cartridges he had purchased and ripped it open. Hurrying, he refilled the weapon's magazine. He felt better after that; the long gun and the pistol together gave him almost two dozen rounds before he would be forced to reload.

Ahead, Kate halted and turned toward him. "We can't go any farther. There's a cliff."

He trotted to her side. He had feared that this would happen, but he had not expected it so quickly. Pausing, he gauged the towering rock wall. It was out of the question. He looked then at the canyon. There was no escape from the ledge by that route either; the slope had become sheer, studded with jagged, finger-like formations of sandstone.

Desperate, he spun and considered the trail ten feet above them. The intervening slope, while steep, was smooth except for a few storm-rounded boulders and clumps of oak brush and rabbitbush. On the trail itself he could see more sandstone upthrusts and scattered junipers. He glanced at Kate.

"It's try to make it up that—or stand against the Apaches."

Her answer was unfaltering. "I'd rather try."

He nodded and wheeled toward the chestnut. Sliding the rifle back into the boot, he unhooked the coil of rope hanging from the saddle. There was no time to spare, but he spent a moment looking toward the canyon. No Indians were in sight; they were still behind the shoulder of rock and below the ledge.

"I'll go first," he said, shaking out a loop. "When I get on top, I'll toss you the lasso. Take a dally around your saddle horn and head the horse up the slope. Once he starts, grab his tail and hang on."

He hesitated a moment to be sure she understood. Then he wheeled and threw his loop for the largest of the rocky fingers above. It caught on the first try. He threw his weight against it, found it solid. Moving then to the gelding, he passed the free end of the rope through the fork of the saddle to form a guy. It was not the best arrangement, but he preferred breaking the hull to choking the chestnut.

Hooking the remainder of the coil over his left shoulder and grasping the ends of the reins, he cast a final glance down the trail, saw no one, and started up the grade.

Slipping, scrambling, clawing, he gained half the distance to the top; then the gelding's reins checked him. He was short of where he had hoped to be, but there was nothing he could do about it.

Bracing himself, he tugged at the leathers and yelled a command at the big horse. The chestnut began to prance about at the foot of the slope, pawing nervously at the incline. Sanderson put his weight against the rope, drew it taut, and gave the reins several hard jerks. The gelding took an experimental step, then balked.

"Slap him!" Sanderson shouted. "Hit him with something!"

Kate picked up a short length of wood and struck the animal sharply on the rump. The horse's hindquarters lowered as he went into a crouch. He lunged up the slope, stabbing at the uncertain surface with his hoofs as he fought to stay upright.

Frank, keeping the guy rope taut, steadied the gelding as best he could, all the while tugging at the reins. The horse's churning hoofs found purchase. He surged upward, slipped, and went to his knees. There was a clatter of gravel as he recovered his footing and moved on.

A chorus of yells sounded along the rim of the canyon. Rifles began to crackle. The sudden reports, the whine of ricocheting bullets screaming off into space were all the gelding needed. With three powerful lunges, he gained the top. Sanderson, caught by the unexpected slack in the rope, went sprawling.

Dangerously close to the horse's driving

hoofs, he rolled away, bounded to his feet, and followed the gelding to the trail. Drawing his revolver, he threw two hasty shots down the slope at the oncoming Apaches. He could see three in the open. There would be more beyond them, judging from the shouting. He watched those in the lead duck to the side as bullets kicked dust around them, then turned his attention to Kate.

"Grab it!" he said, tossing the free end of the rope down to her.

Seizing the riata, she frowned. "My horse—"

"Forget him. We'd never get him up here now."

She wrapped the rope about her waist and began the ascent. Sanderson helped, drawing her up, hand over hand. The moment she was beside him, he stepped to the gelding and obtained his rifle.

"Take the horse and move on. I'll be right behind you.

She snatched at the chestnut's reins and started up the trail, steep but not difficult. Frank dropped back, crouched in the protection of a large rock. The Apaches would have to climb over the rim almost directly below.

A head appeared, the sun shining dully on black, coarse hair, and then a face daubed with red and yellow paint. Sanderson leveled the rifle and squeezed off a shot. Head and face disappeared in an explosion of dirt and rock chips.

As the echoes rolled, more heads appeared.

Grimly, and with methodical accuracy, Sanderson blasted them from the edge of the canyon. He waited out a long minute while the dust cleared. No more warriors were attempting to gain the ledge.

He wondered if that were the last of it; repulsed, would the Apaches try again—or would they leave the canyon and circle around in an effort to head Kate and him off on the mountain? He decided it was foolish to wait and see.

Coming to his feet, he spun and started up the trail at a run. A hundred yards ahead he caught sight of Kate and the chestnut, winding in and out of the rocks. Beyond them hung clear, open sky. A long breath of relief passed through his lips. At least they were out of Calaveras Canyon.

CHAPTER NINTEEN

They did not halt until they were far down the slope of the adjacent mountain and well hidden in a dense thicket. There Frank Sanderson went over the chestnut gelding carefully, examining him to see if he had been injured in any way during the escape from the canyon. Except for a few minor abrasions, the horse was unharmed.

Worn, fighting sleep and denying himself the luxury of stretching out for a few minutes in the shade, be doubled back to a point along the trail

from which he could keep an eye on the sur-
rounding country. He was not convinced the
Apaches had given up, and he was taking no
chances.

For a time Kate rested. Then she roused, went
half-heartedly through the motions of repairing
her appearance, and made her way to where
Sanderson was hunched, his back to a stump,
staring off toward the canyon. Her need for
sleep also was reflected in the weary detach-
ment with which she considered all things.

Few words had passed between them since
they had begun the climb out of the canyon;
seemingly, few had been necessary. But now it
was evident that she had something on her mind
that required discussion. He recognized this as
she settled down beside him.

"We're in a bad way, aren't we?" she said
quietly. It was more a statement of fact than a
question. "We're a long ways from any settlement. No food—and only one horse to carry
us."

The lawman scrubbed at his jaw. "Could be
worse. Chestnut can carry double if we don't
crowd him."

"But—if the Apaches follow us?"

"Maybe they won't."

"You think they will, though, don't you?"

He stirred impatiently. "Who knows what an
Indian's liable to do? Half the time they don't
know themselves. One thing—they'll go a bit
slow trying to crawl over that rim again."

Kate frowned, not understanding. He remembered then that she had not been there when he had driven them back into the canyon. It was just as well.

"Won't they circle around, try to cut us off?"

Sanderson nodded. "But they'll have to go back for their horses. Probably left them on the yonder side of the canyon."

"Then shouldn't we start? I'm all right now."

"Not you I'm thinking about—it's the chestnut. Needs rest. Tough job ahead of him."

Kate fell silent. The sun was climbing steadily. Its hot rays were now drilling into the mountain, turning the slabs of rock again into islands of blistering stone.

"What about Billy Farr? He'll be getting farther away."

She was still thinking of the gold. He guessed that if the earth opened suddenly and swallowed them both, she'd continue to think about it—all the way to hell.

"What about him?" he answered, sourly.

"You said we might find his trail—"

He turned and regarded her closely. "Gold really mean that much to you?"

She met his gaze with steady eyes. "It does. I've explained why. Not so much for me as for my daughter."

Sanderson shrugged. "He'll be heading back the way we came—that much I'm sure." Then he added, "You forgetting Mendoza? He could have got away from the Apaches."

122

"I'm not interested in Mendoza, or anyone else. And I'll worry about them if and when we see them. It's Billy I'm thinking of."

"You want to hunt him down?"

She nodded. "Can we?"

"If that's what you want—we can try."

"It's what I want," she said firmly. "Will it be hard to track him?"

"Shouldn't be. He's got to cross the same country we do. And he'll head for Mexico. Seemed to think that was the answer to everything."

"But his girl—he said she was in Mesilla. That's east of here."

"Could've been just talk. A lot of words to throw us off. May not even be a girl."

"You don't think he stumbled onto us by accident?" The lawman laughed. "He was lying from the start. Figured he was then—dead sure of it now."

"But how—"

"Probably heard about the gold your husband cached, kept an eye on you until you started after it, then followed. He watched his chances, then finally come busting into our camp with that cooked-up yarn he told us."

"It was just a scheme to get the treasure? He wasn't looking for a job, or anything like that?"

"No. And things panned out good for him. He couldn't have known about the Apaches, of course, but their showing up was a break for him. Saved him from having to put a bullet in us."

Kate London stared off into the distance. She closed her eyes tightly and shook her head slowly. "Apaches," she murmured. "I'll never forget those few minutes there in that clearing. We can thank that Mexican captain and his men for showing up when they did."

A faint smile tugged at Sanderson's lips. Kate was capable of the more tender sensibilities after all. "Hope they made it to the flat," he said, pulling himself upright. Extending his hand, he helped her rise. "Time we moved on."

"Are we going straight to Whiterock?" she asked as they walked toward the chestnut.

"Too far. Without water and grub we'd never make it. We'll swing south to Bear Springs first."

"And then?"

He knew what it was that burned at her, pushed her so relentlessly. It angered him. He said, "We'll go after your gold, but we can't do it on one horse."

"Where can we get another?"

"Whiterock—if we have no luck at the Springs. There's a chance we'll find Neff's horse still there."

"I'd forgotten about him. That would save us a lot of time."

He nodded. "Horse won't stray from good grass and water. Probably right where we left him."

"I hope so." She took him by the arm. "Now

124

that it's settled—that's we're going to find Billy, I mean—I want to change our deal. You're to get more of the treasure, not just fifteen hundred dollars. There'll be plenty for Marguerite and me."

Again he was angered. "You don't have to raise the ante. I said I'd go through with it."

"I know, but I want you to have it. You've more than earned a bigger share."

He was silent for a time. Then "Suit yourself," he said, and he moved on to where the gelding waited.

They began the descent of the slope, following a faded trail that had all but disappeared from disuse. Sanderson no longer bothered to watch the ridge behind them. If the Apaches planned to pursue, they would not come from that direction now. If there were to be trouble, he could expect them when they reached the flat.

He led the gelding. He did not offer to let Kate ride, simply permitting her to walk, as he did. He knew she was tired, that with each successive step she was becoming more thirsty and in need of food. But he knew also that the strength of the big horse had to be conserved; it would be needed later. Thus he hardened himself to the thought of what Kate was going through.

They drew near the foot of the slope where it broadened into a wide saddle and spilled onto the plain. Avoiding such open country, Frank crossed to the far side while they were still under cover of brush. If the Apaches were there, he didn't intend to walk into their arms blindly.

At the end of the brush he called a halt. Leaving Kate and the chestnut behind, he went on, seeking out a high point from which he could probe the area thoroughly. He spent a full half-hour at the chore, but saw no indication of Indians or anyone else. Finally satisfied there was no danger, he returned, and once again they moved on.

They broke out onto the flat a mile below the saddle. Frank glanced at Kate. She was at the point of collapse. He wheeled the gelding broadside to her and helped her to mount.

"We'll ride from here on."

She sighed deeply as she settled in the saddle. Sanderson, no less grateful, mounted behind her.

"How far to the Springs?" she asked when they were under way. "I've never been so thirsty."

"Be there by dark," he replied, gauging the sun. "Unless we run into trouble."

Luck was with them. Shortly after sundown they reached the upper end of the jutting peninsula of trees and undergrowth. They entered slowly, Sanderson still cautious after their encounter with the Apaches. The gelding too seemed nervous. He continually flicked his ears forward and threw up his head as if endeavoring to see into the shadowy brush.

126

When they were within a dozen strides of the spring, Sanderson halted and slipped from the gelding's back. An odd feeling that all was not right plucked at his consciousness, alerted his nerves. Drawing his pistol, he moved on, then pulled up short. There were several horses at the pool. And one of their pack mules....

CHAPTER TWENTY

Crouched low, Sanderson worked in nearer, then stopped again. Raising his head, he peered through the screen of brush. Satisfaction filled him. They had caught up with Billy Farr. Or had they?

He could see only one of the missing mules. Neff's sorrel stood a short distance below him, and on the opposite side of the small stream were two more horses, both saddled and bridled. He had not seen them before.

Frank dropped back and circled, intending to come in from behind the animals for a better look. The sickening odor of putrefying flesh assailed his nostrils. He halted and wheeled slowly. A few paces away, the bodies of two men lay partly hidden in the undergrowth.

Restraining an impulse to investigate, Sanderson moved on, continuing his search of the area. There was no one else around. Farr had apparently transferred his load to one mule, abandoned the other, and kept going.

He retraced his steps to the dead men. Approaching upwind, be knelt beside them and rolled them to their backs. Coyotes had been at the bodies, but he was able to recognize one—an outlaw named Con Fallon. The other was a stranger. They had been killed by blows that had crushed their skulls, and they had been dead several days.

Sanderson pulled back. Evidently the two horses still wearing gear belonged to them; and whoever had murdered them—while they slept evidently, as their blankets were beneath them—had moved on in a hurry.

Farr?

It could not have been Billy. At least, it could not have been his work during the return flight with the gold. Fallon and his partner had been dead longer than that. But earlier—a few days earlier…Frank recalled the different dust clouds he had watched as he and his party hurried toward Calaveras Canyon. First there had been three, one of which could be attributed to the Rurales.

And then there had been only two, as if one group of riders had halted—or perhaps united with the other. Sanderson considered that. Had Fallon and his friend, also in pursuit of Kate London and the gold, accidentally met Billy Farr, somewhere near the Springs? And then later, becoming aware of their purpose and determined to share the treasure with no one, had

128

Billy killed them as they slept?

It was pure speculation—but the pieces fitted. Billy, ridding himself of competition, had then ridden on, later to present himself and his story of fear at Kate London's camp. There was proof of none of it—but it all made sense.

Rising, he paused to quench his thirst; then, crossing the stream, he gathered up the reins of the loose horses and led them back to where Neff's sorrel and the mule grazed. Moving to where he could sec Kate, he signaled for her to come in.

She halted near the water, immediately went to her knees, and slaked her thirst. Looking up, she saw the animals. Her expression changed. "Billy?"

"Been here and gone. Put everything he wanted on one mule and the horse he was riding."

Kate rose slowly. "Anyway—we found the sorrel." She frowned. "Those other horses. Who—"

"Two men dead over there in the brush. Both outlaws, I expect."

She stared at him. "You think Billy—"

The lawman shrugged. "Be my guess. No way to be sure."

She turned wearily toward him. "I'm glad we found the sorrel. Won't have to waste time riding to Whiterock. Are we going to keep right after Billy?"

"We're in no shape to do that, and you know

it," be said wearily. "Got to get some rest—and we need some food in our bellies."

"But he's probably close!"

"Not close enough to help much. That gold's set him on fire; he's on a dead run. We'll be smart to bed down for the night, get an early start in the morning. We'll be in shape to travel fast while he'll have to slow down."

Kate London nodded, recognizing the logic of it. She glanced around. "What can I do?"

"See if you can find some grub. Look in that pack on the mule—and in the saddlebags of the horses; might scare up a little. Soon as I'm finished I'll give you a hand."

She looked at him questioningly. He motioned toward the brush.

"Got to bury Fallon and his friend. That wind shifts, we won't be able to stay around here."

"Fallon?" she repeated, and then, realizing, she lowered her head and moved away.

Sanderson glanced about the camp. There was nothing he could use as a spade. He crossed to where the bodies lay. He'd just have to cover them with litter and rocks. It was the best he could do.

Finished, he returned to the clearing. Kate, near exhaustion, was sitting on a log next to the small stream.

"Find anything?" he asked.

She stirred. "Nothing. He took everything but some cook pots and the blankets."

"How about the saddlebags?"

"They've been emptied. By him, I guess."

Sanderson obtained his rifle. "Means I'll have to rustle us up a rabbit or two," he said, trying to be cheerful about it, and strode off into the brush.

He killed a long-eared jack just at dark. He regretted the sound of the gunshot, since it could betray their presence to anyone who might be searching for them, but food was a necessity. Back in camp, he skinned the lean-bodied animal and put it to roasting over a low fire. While he performed that chore, Kate prepared pallets, using the blankets left in the pack of the abandoned mule.

They ate in silence, having nothing but the tough, stringy meat and fresh water to make up the meal, but it satisfied the gnawing hunger pains in their stomachs and eased them considerably. When it was over, Kate, almost asleep on her feet, turned in at once. Sanderson, after killing the fire, turned to the horses.

He picketed Neff's sorrel with his own chestnut, making certain they could not get loose and stray, and then removed the gear from the mule and the horses that had belonged to Con Fallon and his partner, allowing them their freedom. Then taking up the blankets Kate London had spread for him, and with his rifle in hand, he walked a short distance to the edge of the flat.

There he found a slight rise that permitted him to look out over the country lying between the Springs and the mountains and settled down. If the Apaches—or Pablo Mendoza—were on their trail, they would come from that direction. The Rurale, of course, would present no problem once he knew they had no gold. But the Apaches were a different story.

Around him the small sounds of the night had hushed. Now, as he became quiet, they resumed, presenting a cacophony of clicking insects, chirpings, and the rustlings of small animals in the dry leaves. Coyotes yelped from the distant slopes, and he found that comforting and reassuring. He should rest—but somehow he was ill at ease.

He stirred restlessly. His eyes were heavy, and weariness was a dull ache throughout his body. It seemed weeks since he'd slept. A warm breeze sprang up and brushed lightly against his face. More coyotes had joined the raucous serenade in the hills, and it seemed now that they were strung the entire length of the range.

An old saw trickled through his mind: *When coyotes howl, only the wildfolk prowl.* It was true, he thought. He could sleep. No one was abroad in the silver-shot night....

He awoke suddenly, a deep-seated alarm pushing at him. He sat perfectly still, rifle across his knees, listening into the hush. Something had aroused him—just what he could not be sure. And then he knew. The barking along the Peloncillos had ceased. It was the very silence that had aroused him.

Getting to his feet, he glanced to the east,

132

wondering how long he had slept. Several hours probably, but there was still no beginning haze of daylight. He swung his eyes to the north and scanned the flat. Nothing. Only the eerie, pale land rising and falling under the starshine. But something was wrong.

Delaying no longer, he wheeled and hurried back to camp. He glanced at Kate London, sleeping the sleep of the utterly exhausted. He disliked awakening her, but they'd be fools to take a chance. He would wait until the last moment. Moving to where the chestnut and Neff's sorrel dozed, he quickly threw their gear into place and, filling both canteens from the spring, led the horses to where Kate lay.

She sat up instantly at his touch. "What is it?"

"We're moving out."

Immediately she began drawing on her boots and the light jacket she had brought. "Is there something wrong?" she asked, rising.

"Somebody's coming—headed this way from the mountains."

"Who?"

He shook his head. "Can't tell. Fact is, I don't even see them. But they're out there."

She questioned him no further, knowing he would make no such unexpected move without cause. She crossed to where her horse waited.

Sanderson helped her into the saddle and swung onto the chestnut. Immediately he turned into the brush.

To head due south would be smart, since it would place the long, narrow finger of trees and undergrowth between them and whoever it was riding in from the Peloncillos.

"What about finding Billy's trail?"

Temper and the imminence of danger sharpened his tongue. "The hell with Billy's trail!" he snapped. Then he regretted his harsh words. "Plenty of time. We'll start looking soon as it's light."

They pressed on, holding the horses to a steady lope. An hour later they were in the open with no brush to conceal their passage. Sanderson's hope then was that they were far enough from the spring to be out of sight when their pursuers reached that point.

The miles slipped by. The warm breeze faded, changing to a cool wind blowing out of the west. Light began to show in the eastern sky, finally becoming a gray line that turned gradually into a yellow haze shot with fingers of orange. Sanderson began to watch their back trail. The country and its landmarks were distinct now—and they were still alone.

Just after dawn, his glance picked up a scarring on a slope to their left. He veered from course and rode in for a closer look. A hard grin cracked his lips as he beckoned to Kate. When she was at his side, he pointed to the imprints in the loose sand.

"Farr," he said. "A horse and a mule made those."

He raised his eyes and followed the tracks as far as he could distinguish them. "Run due south—for Mexico."

Kate brightened. "Then he's not far ahead. We've got a chance to overtake him."

Frank Sanderson had twisted about on his saddle and was staring off in the direction of the Springs. "Not all we got," he said, squaring himself. "That's dust behind us."

CHAPTER TWENTY-ONE

Kate whirled. A tautness gripped her features. She studied the cloud for a moment, then asked, "Do you think they've seen us?"

"We raise dust, same as they do," he replied, and he put the gelding into motion.

It was a grim game now; the fleeing Billy Farr followed by them; they, in turn, pursued by someone else, identity yet unknown. When and where the chase would end, and its outcome, was anybody's guess.

Riding Farr's tracks, they hurried on through the morning hours. By noon the heat had become intense. The sun, a circle of glaring, white fire creeping across a steel arch, bore down with merciless fury. There was not the faintest wisp of breeze, and the land into which they were entering was a glittering, limitless void. There was little brush to be seen, and that was con-

135

fined to small clumps of snakeweed, an occasional sand hummock of mesquite or creosote bush, and gaunt, spiny-armed chollas.

Sanderson, an arm's length from Kate, watched her brush at the circles of sweat gathered on her cheeks and neck. He could not blame her for wanting to live in a kinder world—one where her Marguerite could enjoy a more genteel life. He understood, but he could not agree. Despite the bitter turn his own fortunes had taken, he could visualize no satisfaction for himself anywhere except in the west.

It was a raw country, fit only for those willing to accept it on its own terms. And it would remain so, for it was peopled by a rough lot—men like Virg Peck and Con Fallon and Harvey Neff; even Billy Farr. And their kind didn't die easily. As long as their like remained to haunt the hills and ride the flats, the land would still be violent and untamed.

He was a part of that restless, free society, he realized. Once he had been of the opposition— one of the civilizers—but that had ended. Had he felt remorse at the change? Frank Sanderson didn't really know.

Near the middle of the afternoon, the horses began to show the effects of the grueling pace. Spotting a palo verde tree in a shallow wash, the lawman angled to it and halted in its filigree shadow. There was no escape from the brutal heat or the glare of the sand, but there was a suggestion of shade, and for that they were

136

grateful.

Kate, her back resting against the slim green trunk of the palo verde, loosened her shirt and fanned herself languidly with her hat. From its shelter beneath a rock, a whip-tailed lizard clicked noisily.

"I don't see how anything can live out here," she murmured.

Sanderson hunched on his heels and looked off to the north. The dust cloud was still there. "Nothing gets around in the heat of the day. Things come alive at night. Man has a choice, he ought to be smart and wait until then too."

"We didn't have that choice," she said.

He shrugged. After a moment he rose, took one of the canteens from his saddle, and offered it to her. She had her drink. He permitted himself a swallow and then, soaking his handkerchief, he squeezed a quantity into the mouth of each horse and wiped their nostrils and lips. That done, he resumed his position. The small effort expended had brought sweat to his face. He brushed it off with a forearm.

"You're wondering if this is all worth what we're going through," Kate said, picking up the thread of the conversation.

"Something for you to decide."

She gave him a worn, smile. "To me it is. You'd have to be a woman, go through what I have, to understand that."

"Even the lives of a half a dozen men?"

She looked away. "No one forced them to get

137

involved. They did it on their own. Just as you…

He had no answer to that. Then, "What about Farr? He's not going to just fork over that gold when we catch up."

"He made that choice, too—stealing it from me. He'll have to expect the consequences."

Sanderson shifted and looked again to the north. The roll was a bit larger. "Then I guess you figure it's worth the cost."

"Is that so wrong?"

"Wouldn't know," he answered impatiently. "To me, gold is gold—something you use when you've got it and do without when you haven't."

She looked at him curiously. "You mean you've never felt the need to have everything you want—just anything that struck your fancy?"

"Never gave it much thought. Good life comes from being alive, having a full belly, and something to do."

"There's more to it than that. Better things—"

"How can you tell what's better?" he broke in. "How do you know? You seem to think money makes the difference. I don't. Man with a lot of cash has a lot of worries. One without, like me, doesn't. All he needs do is live, enjoy what comes his way."

Kate smiled. "You sound as if you're trying to convince yourself, not me. I wonder if you felt that way before the trouble in Kansas

138

Bend."

His eyes flared with surprise and anger. He reached down for a handful of sand, allowed it to spill through his fingers.

"Could be that's what changed my thinking—made me realize how a man can work like hell all his life for nothing."

"Maybe only you look at it that way. What really happened?"

He flung the remainder of the sand to one side.

"Not worth the telling."

"I'd like to hear it."

He rode out a long minute debating the matter with himself, then finally nodded. "Was the marshal there—in Kansas Bend. Had been for several years. Kept a good, clean town and everybody knew it. One day a stranger blew in, got busy opening up a new place. Seemed to have plenty of money, and it was a right fancy layout—saloon, gambling rooms, dance hall, girls—the whole thing.

"Nothing wrong with that; town had no law against such places long as they played it square. That's what caused the trouble. Didn't take me long to find out Corbin—the man who owned the outfit—was running a crook joint. He had the finest collection of cold-deckers I've ever run across.

"I closed him down. There was quite a holler, but I made it stick until he agreed to get rid of his sharpies and run an honest game. He opened

139

up again, and in less than a week I saw that nothing had changed. It was the same old thing, only with a new bunch standing behind the tables. I told him to lock up—and stay locked up.

"Next thing I knew, he'd gone to the mayor and some of the businessmen and told them he'd been paying me off on the side—that I'd shut him down because I'd raised the ante and he couldn't afford to pay."

Kate leaned forward. "They believed him?"

"Corbin made it easy for them. He put a hundred dollars in gold pieces into a Bull Durham sack and managed somehow to slip it into the drawer of my desk.

Then he invited them to take a look. Said it was his proof."

"And that was the end of it."

Sanderson scooped up another handful of sand. "No—they swallowed his yarn, all right. It bothered me plenty, and I made them go with me while I called him a liar to his face. Things got a bit nasty, and he stuck his hand inside his coat for something. I thought he was reaching for a gun. I killed him.

"That topped it off. They were sure then he was telling the truth. I handed over my star and walked out. They didn't have any real proof that I'd taken Corbin's bribe. And far as the shooting was concerned, most everybody figured same as I did—and I had the right to protect myself...."

"Did you ever go back?"

He shook his head. "Heard later one of Corbin's girls admitted putting that money in my desk for him, but it didn't mean anything to me then."

"It should. You ought to return. Your name's clear now."

"Now is too late. Right then is when it counted. They should have believed me after all the time I'd put in working for them. I figure I was entitled to a little more faith and trust."

Kate London sighed. "People are only human, Frank. Believe me—I know. They all make mistakes—even those we think shouldn't. You have to make allowances—"

"No!" he snapped, suddenly angered. "They're the ones who were wrong—not me. And that's the way it can stay. I don't give a damn if—"

"Of course you do!" she broke in. "Men and their pride—you're all such fools! Go back—those people in Kansas Bend probably feel worse about it than you. Give them and yourself a chance. Make a new start."

He shook his head stubbornly. "They had a chance."

"But it's different now. And this isn't the kind of life you want. I know it—and you know it. Sticks out all over you. Why—you despise it, same as you despise the men like Neff and Peck and Billy Farr who are part of it. Why can't you see that?"

He stared at her for the space of a breath;

then he got to his feet. "Way things are suits me," he said. He glanced over his shoulder. The dust had grown in size.

They had wasted far too much time. "Let's move out."

Saying nothing, she allowed him to assist her onto the sorrel. As he was climbing onto the gelding, she had her look at the yellowish pall.

"Do you think it's the Apaches?"

"Could be. Or maybe Mendoza."

"We don't have to fear him. We haven't got the gold. He could search us, find out."

"But he'd guess we were chasing somebody that does have it, and hang around. Best we try to lose him."

They struck off in the withering heat. Who-ever it was—Rurales or Indians—Sanderson noted, was not riding hard. The cloud moved slowly, if steadily, and he gauged their own pace accordingly to conserve the horses.

A mile later, Kate broke the silence. "How far are we from the border?"

"Never been across here. I'd guess we're fairly close."

"Will we be safe once we reach it?"

"Might stop the Apaches. If it's Mendoza, he'll be right at home."

Kate, looking straight ahead, raised herself slightly. "There's something down there— below us. In that little valley. Houses, I think. Or maybe it's just the sun—a mirage."

Sanderson squinted into the glare. "Houses,

sure enough. Maybe a town. Farr probably stopped there." He threw a glance at the persistent dust cloud. "Could be we'll be losing them now."

CHAPTER TWENTY-TWO

An hour later, they halted at the edge of the settlement—no more than two squalid shacks and a combination saloon and general store. Sanderson swore in disgust. If there were Apaches moving in on them, they could expect no help here. He assessed the small settlement in a single look.

"No sign of Farr. Let's pick up some grub and ask a few questions, then move on."

They rode up to the hitch rack fronting the store and dismounted. Crossing the porch, they entered the dingy, cluttered room, rank with the odor of rancid meat and musty flour. An elderly, unshaven man wearing steel-rimmed spectacles, collarless shirt, and ragged overalls greeted them unsmilingly.

"Something you're wanting?"

Sanderson said, "Grub—and information."

The old man was raking Kate London with bright, appreciative eyes. Sanderson took a step toward him. He straightened hurriedly.

"Reckon I got the grub," he mumbled.

"The information too, probably. Aim to pay

for both."

The storekeeper folded his arms across his chest. "What's on your mind, mister?"

"Looking for a friend. Probably passed here yesterday. Be riding a buckskin and leading a mule."

The man grinned, exposing toothless gums. "Billy Farr?"

"That's him."

"Sure; he was here. Sold him a horse and some trappings."

Sanderson frowned. "The buckskin play out?"

"Nope. Needed it for his wife."

Sanderson hid his surprise. "Forgot about her. She been waiting here for him long?"

"Come in on the stage, four—five days ago. Rented herself a room out back."

The lawman glanced at Kate. It was as he had thought: Farr had planned from the beginning— even to having his girl waiting for him at the border way station. He had been sure of himself—very sure.

"Right nice boy, that Billy," the old man said. "And his missus—pretty as a picture."

"For a fact," Sanderson agreed. "How long ago did they pull out for Mexico? We been trying to catch up."

"Was early this morning. Be no chore catching them; they was only going far as San Miguel. You say you wanted some groceries?"

Frank Sanderson inclined his head toward

Kate. "Lady knows what she wants."

He turned, sauntered idly to the window, and looked out through streaky, fly-specked glass. The dust cloud was nearer and definitely angling toward them. Vaguely he heard Kate naming off the articles she wished—with the exception of coffee, all prepared food that would require no cooking.

He thought of Farr. San Miguel, the storekeeper had said, was where he intended to halt. Sanderson had no idea where it lay or how large it might be. It could be just another wide place in the road, such as this. It didn't matter—except that if it were a town of size, there would be Rurales....

He heard the storekeeper name his price for the supplies and reached into his pocket for the necessary coins. As he tossed them onto the counter, he saw the old man's face register disappointment.

"Something wrong?"

"Silver. Was hoping you'd be paying in gold—same as Billy."

"I'm saving mine," Sanderson said, and picking up the flour sack, he slung it over his shoulder. "How far to San Miguel—and which way?"

The old man cocked his head slyly. "You only paid for the grub, mister."

The lawman dropped another silver dollar onto the counter—his last. "You're paid now."

"You want to ride all night, you can make it

by sunup. Just keep heading down the valley till you come to the end of the trees. Trail forks; take the right hand."

Sanderson swung about and waited until Kate had moved in front of him; then together they retraced their steps to the horses. He stowed the supplies in her saddlebags, holding out some of the hard biscuits, dried meat, and two cans of peaches to eat as they traveled.

They rode out immediately, and for a time, while they satisfied their hunger, there was silence between them. Finally, Kate spoke.

"You had everything figured right about Billy."

"Everything but the girl. Had my doubts there was one. He was plenty sure he'd pull it off— having her waiting here for him."

"Like Peck said—it's easy to be certain when you're young." She paused, noticing him turn and look back. "They still following us?"

He nodded. "Gaining some—and they're slanting in. Could be they figure to cut us off before we reach the border."

"Can they?" There was a note of alarm in her voice.

He tossed away the empty peach tin. "Hard to say. Don't know how far we are from the line. We can hold our own. Their horses have covered the same miles ours have; they'll be in no better shape."

"Then—if we don't stop—"

"Have to—somewhere along the way. Horse

can only take so much without rest."

"But, can't we try—just keep going? We're so close now..."

"Be fools to run the horses into the ground. On foot we'd be a long time reaching that town." He looked at her closely. "Don't worry; we'll make it."

Kate settled back with a sigh. She dabbed at the sweat on her tanned face. "Everything takes so long," she murmured. "Seems we move so slow..."

"Better be hoping Billy's slow about spending that gold. Ought to have more sense than use it, at least for a while."

"Why?" she asked, wonderingly.

"The Mexican government'll have every soldier and politician in the country on the watch for it. Farr starts throwing it around in San Miguel, he'll bring the Rurales down on his neck in a hurry. They could beat us to him."

That stirred an immediate fear within her. "I—I wish we could move faster!"

"After dark, when it's cooler, we can."

They reached the end of the trees and veered to the right. Ahead the land lay raw and broken, a limitless sun-swept plain gashed by arroyos and low, ragged buttes. They pushed on, bearing directly into the center of it as the heat seemed to mount.

For hours there was little variation, and then the trail dropped off in a steep slope into a broad mesquite-choked wash. The ground lost its firmness and became a nightmare of loose sand. Both horses began to labor, lunge as if bucking snowdrifts. Sanderson and Kate London dismounted and led the animals, now covered with lather and sucking deeply for wind.

A short time later the trail lifted and climbed to a higher level, and the soil became more solid. To their right Sanderson saw a low bluff where a strip of shade was beginning to broaden. He moved toward it.

"We're resting there," he said, his tone making it plain he would brook no opposition. "Soon as it's sundown, we'll go on."

CHAPTER TWENTY-THREE

They traveled throughout the night without incident and crossed the border early the next morning. Farther to the west, in the direction of towering Chiricahua Peak, the dust cloud had also progressed southward.

Kate London, following Sanderson's pointing finger with heavy eyes, stirred wearily. "I'd hoped they'd stop—that we'd seen the last of them."

He studied the yellow boil thoughtfully. It was nearer. He could make out two, maybe three riders; there could be more. "They've guessed we're headed for San Miguel. They're swinging this way."

148

"But Apaches—would they try—"

"Maybe they're not Apaches."

She turned to him. "But if they're not—who are they? Outlaws?"

He shrugged. "Anybody's guess. Point is, we've got to reach the town ahead of them."

His head came up abruptly as they broke out onto a rim below which a narrow, treeless valley spread. Kate pulled up beside him quickly.

"Is—is that it—San Miguel?"

"Must be. Didn't expect it so close to the line."

There was relief in Kate London's voice. "Then we beat them. We'll find Billy first."

Frank Sanderson was not listening; he was studying the town with deliberate care. It was not large—two dozen or so sun-baked huts, all of unplastered adobe bricks; a church; a corral; three or four one-story buildings. There appeared to be one street that followed no particular course and numerous short alleys that intersected at irregular intervals. A small stream cut a meandering path along its eastern edge.

Not many persons were abroad, and those who were moved about with little enthusiasm as they followed the custom of accomplishing necessary chores before the intense heat set in.

"Won't be hard, finding Billy," the lawman said, putting the chestnut into motion. "But we'll have to take it easy. Be a lot better if it was still dark."

"We're strangers. Why would they bother

149

us?"

"They won't bother us, but the news that more gringos have come to town will spread in a hurry. Billy's sure to overhear."

They reached a break in the rim and began a steady drop to the floor of the valley. There was no cover of consequence that would mask their approach, and Sanderson pointed the gelding for the blind corner of the nearest structure.

Kate, riding close beside him, said, "What do you plan to do—try at every house?"

He shook his head, "Just look for the buck-skin and the mule. There'll be another horse—the one the girl's riding."

They gained the rear of the hut, Sanderson cut in behind it, and they continued slowly along the rear of the houses. There were few sheds, and only once did Frank wheel in to have a closer look at a possibility. He found the structure empty.

Coming to the end of the town, they crossed over and started back along the opposite side. A woman washing clothes glanced curiously at them as they passed. Sanderson spoke, but she did not reply. He glanced at the eastern sky. It was growing late, and the need to locate Farr before the entire settlement was up and about was pressing him urgently.

A dog rushed from the rear of a house and set up a furious barking, spooking Kate's sorrel to a quick trot. She pulled down the horse and waited for Sanderson to catch up. Somewhere in

150

the village a tardy rooster began to crow. And then, at the fourth hut from the end, they found that for which they searched.

In an act typical of his disregard for horse-flesh, Farr had left his animals standing, still with gear, at a hitch rack. Heads swung low, they dozed patiently. Only the mule had been unloaded. From that Sanderson judged that Billy had spent the night, or most of it, in the shack.

He considered the low-roofed structure for several minutes. A door and a single window faced them from the rear. The front arrangement would be similar. He could expect the sides to have small openings, but only for the purpose of ventilation. The lawman, pondering the problem of choice, decided upon the rear. Farr, if given a chance to run, would make a dash for the horses.

Dismounting, he tied the gelding to a clump of greasewood behind the adjacent house, Kate followed suit. Drawing his pistol, he checked the cylinder, then glanced at her.

"Best you wait here."

Her answer was firm. "I'm going with you."

There was no time to argue the matter. Removing his spurs, Sanderson crossed to the back of the hut, Kate at his heels. They came to the south wall and halted near the open window. A faded cloth curtain blocked their view, but the sound of deep snoring issued from the room.

The lawman edged to the door. Taking the

151

latch handle in his left hand, he tried it gently. The door gave an inch, caught; a strap or a bit of cord, serving as a hook, secured it from the inside. Sanderson pulled back a step. Pistol ready, he raised his leg and drove his boot against the flimsy panel.

It flew in with a splintering crash. Sanderson lunged into the half-dark room, a woman's frightened screams ringing in his ears. He saw Farr and the girl on a pallet along the opposite wall. They leaped upright, Billy throwing himself to one side as he reached for the rifle standing in the corner.

"No!" the lawman shouted.

Billy Farr froze, legs bent, arm extended. He wheeled slowly and faced Sanderson and Kate. His eyes were hard and narrow, his mouth a gray line. There was no boyishness to him now.

Sanderson moved by him cautiously, took possession of the rifle, and retreated to his original position.

"Where's the gold?"

Farr made no reply. Frank looked at the girl. She stood slightly in front of Billy, clutching one of the blankets to her body. Young and pretty in a doll-like way, she showed no fear, only defiance.

"He stole that gold," the lawman said, holding her gaze. "Belongs to this lady here. If you know what he's done with it, tell me. I don't want to kill him."

"That'd be real smart," Farr jeered. "You'd

sure never find it then."

"I would," Sanderson said easily. "You'd not let it get far from you. You're not the trusting kind." Half-turning to Kate, he pointed with the rifle at a jumble of sacks and clothing in the far corner of the musty room. "Take a look. Probably find the saddlebags there."

Kate London did not move. She seemed petrified as she stared at Billy and the girl.

"Kate!"

Still she did not hear. Cursing, Sanderson propped the rifle against the wall behind him and, keeping his pistol leveled at Farr, edged past her. Reaching the corner, be began to probe about in the confused pile with his toe. He touched something solid and worked it into the open. It was one of the saddlebags. The remaining three were there also. He grinned at Farr.

"Like I said, you're not the trusting kind," Sanderson murmured, and he knelt to pick up the pouches.

"You can bet on it!" Billy Farr yelled suddenly, and he shoved the girl straight at Sanderson.

Frank tried to jerk away, but the room was small.

Meg crashed into him. She screamed once as they came together, then began to sob as they went down, her body upon him, smothering his weapon.

Sanderson, scrambling, pushed her aside and bounded upright. There had been no chance to

153

shoot—and now it was too late. Farr, a revolver in his hand, faced him from across the shadowy quarters.

"Should've looked under my blankets, Marshal. Always keep me a gun hid there. Never know when I might need it. Drop that iron to the floor."

Frank allowed his pistol to fall. He looked to Kate. She had stepped back and stood with her shoulders pressed against the door, which had swung shut. The rifle was close. He pointed at the gun angrily.

"Why the hell didn't you grab that—use it?"

She shook her head, and he stared. Something had come over Kate London. She had been so determined, so unrelenting, and now…he stirred impatiently.

"You can kiss your gold good-by," he said, and he turned away.

Farr laughed and crossed in front of her. He picked up the rifle and tossed it onto the pile of blankets. The girl, sobbing quietly, got to her feet. Still covering herself, she moved next to Billy. He grinned at her.

"Maybe I was a mite rough, honey, but I just had to do it. Ain't nobody taking that gold from me."

"Even if you kill her," Sanderson said in disgust. "That gun of mine could've gone off."

"Only it didn't. That's the big difference in us. I ain't afraid to take a chance—and you are. Now suppose you step over there alongside

Missus London, where I can keep an eye on the both of you."

Sanderson moved slowly to where Kate stood. His mind was working rapidly, searching for a way to overcome Farr, regain possession of a weapon, and claim the gold. But Billy was watching him closely.

He still could not understand Kate's actions—or lack of them. She had been insistent they keep after Billy Farr, yet when they had finally cornered him and he needed her most, she had failed him. She was like someone paralyzed, unable to move. He was afraid now to depend on her; if anything was to be done, he must do it alone.

"Get your duds on, honey," he heard Farr say. "Best we pull out of here."

Meg wheeled obediently and picked up her garments. With her back to them, she began to dress. It required only moments. She turned around, now clad in corded, split riding skirt, blouse, and boots. She pulled her dark hair into a bun on the nape of her neck and, holding several pins between her teeth, worked at it until it was firm.

When she had finished, Farr handed her the rifle, its hammer cocked and ready.

"What are we doing with them?" she asked, frowning.

"We're leaving them right here—alive, if they don't get to acting up," Billy replied. He took the rifle from her hand. "Some rope there in that stuff. Give it to me."

The girl backed into the corner and pawed about until she found the coil of hemp.

"Knife on my belt," Farr said, turning partly to her. "Whack us off about four pieces."

In quick, nervous movements, the girl did his bidding. When she had the necessary lengths ready, Billy pressed the rifle back into her hand and took the rope.

"Either one of them makes a move—you shoot," he said in a hard voice. "You understand? Shoot!"

White-lipped, holding the weapon in both hands, Meg nodded.

Farr motioned to Kate and Sanderson. "Turn around; start looking at that wall. Put your hands behind you."

Kate London wheeled woodenly. Frank, still seeking an opening, hesitated. If he could catch Billy off guard for the briefest instant, he would be willing to take a chance. There evidently was some doubt in Farr's mind as to how much he could depend on the girl. That could be the key.

"Use your head, Billy," he said. "Plenty of gold there for all of us. And you'll be needing help to get out of here. Like as not the Rurales've got us spotted by now."

It was a shot in the dark. Farr paused, considering. Then he shrugged. "How the hell would they know about us?"

"People talk. You think nobody saw you ride in here with a mule all loaded down with saddlebags? You think they didn't wonder what was in those bags?"

"Let 'em wonder," Billy snapped. "Now, get yourself turned around there, unless you want me busting your skull with my gun barrel."

"Like you did Con Fallon and his partner?"

Billy Farr grinned and said nothing.

"Better listen to me," Sanderson said, taking up his argument. "Agree to split the gold and we'll ride out together. Doubles your chances of getting away."

"You ain't getting none of it!" Farr shouted, and grasping the lawman's arm, he spun him around and shoved him hard against the wall.

Anger flared through Sanderson. "Better use that gun," he said in a low voice. "Once I'm loose, I'll hunt you down."

"Mexico's a big place."

"Not big enough."

He felt Billy's hands at his wrists, jerking them into position. If he were to make a move, it would have to be now. Whirl. Drive his elbow into the boy's belly....

"You—in the house!"

At the crisp summons, Billy Farr paused. He swore deeply. "Who the hell—"

"This is Captain Mendoza—of the Rurales. You are surrounded. I have no wish to kill, but this I must do unless you surrender!"

CHAPTER TWENTY-FOUR

Mendoza!

Sanderson grinned. The officer hadn't died in Calaveras Canyon after all. And that dust cloud that had haunted Kate and him all the way to the border made sense now. It hadn't been the Apaches, but Mendoza and his men hanging grimly on to the trail of the gold.

"Rurales!" he heard Billy Farr mutter. "What the hell they wanting?"

"Gold," Sanderson replied. "Been on our heels from the start."

"You mean they're the ones back there at the canyon, when the Indians jumped us?"

"The same."

Relief came into Farr's voice. "Well, he's whistling at the moon if he thinks I'm handing the gold over to him. He's only got two men. Maybe not even that. This place ain't surrounded. He's bluffing."

"Don't bet on it. We're in Mexico. Most likely he's scouted up plenty of help." Frank started to turn. Farr's words checked him.

"Keep looking the other way!" Silence followed, and then he said, "Reckon we'll have to run for it, Meg."

"Don't be a fool!" Sanderson warned. "You'll never make it to your horses."

"Figure my luck's still holding."

"Inside the house!" Mendoza's impatient

voice cut into Farr's words. "Come—with the hands up. It is my last time to ask!"

"Help me with the saddlebags," Billy said, ignoring the order. He picked up two of the connected pouches and slung them over his shoulders.

The girl lifted a third, staggering slightly under its weight.

"Come on—goddammit," Farr said peevishly, his nerves suddenly on edge. "Ain't time to fool around."

Meg, apparently unaware of the fourth pair of bags, moved toward the door. Kate turned about slowly, her eyes on the girl.

"Wait—"

The pressure of Farr's gun barrel in Sanderson's back increased. He heard the boy say, "Ready? Now, all we got to do is step out, run for the horses. They's maybe one man out there. I'll take care of him."

Frank, ignoring the pistol, twisted his head around. "Both of you—listen to me. You're dead if you go through that door. I know this Mendoza."

Billy Farr jabbed deep with the gun barrel. A hard grin pulled at his lips as Sanderson flinched. "To hell with you and Mendoza," he said, and he jerked open the door.

The small room was split by a shaft of light. Sanderson pivoted fast, hopeful of stopping the girl. She and Billy Farr were outlined briefly in the framework, and then both were in the open

159

and running. A dozen breathless seconds passed. The hut rocked with the echo of blasting guns.

Kate cried out and started for the door. Sanderson caught her by the arm and roughly dragged her back. "What the hell's the matter with you? Step out there and you're dead as they are!"

"The girl—she—"

"Can't help her now," he said. Two crumpled shapes lay in the dust of the yard. Billy and Meg had covered less than twenty paces when a hail of bullets had cut them down.

Kate London turned back into the room. Outside, excited voices were shouting back and forth. Smoke and the smell of burnt gunpowder hung in the hot air, mingled with the stale odor within the hut.

"Two more dead," Sanderson said in a tense, bitter tone. "Your gold came high. But there's still some left. A whole saddlebag full the girl missed. It's all yours. I'll forget my share."

She did not answer. She continued to stare at the wall.

"Mendoza doesn't know how much we brought out of the Canyon. He'll think that's all of it, out there on the ground with Billy and the girl. I'll tell him nothing, one way or the other. It'll be a lie, but I gave you my word I'd help you—and I'll keep it."

Kate London came around slowly and faced him. "I—I don't want it, Frank."

160

A wild fury rushed through him. "You *what*? We sweat out more'n a week in hell—we've got dead people strung from here to the end of the Peloncillos—and now you don't want it! I—"

"You don't understand. There's no need, no reason. That girl—Meg. She was my daughter...."

Sanderson's jaw sagged. Kate turned and with unseeing eyes stared through the open doorway.

"I thought I recognized her. Later I was sure. There was a birthmark on her arm. And she looked like Dandy—like her father. After I saw her—somehow the gold didn't matter any more..."

"For the love of God," Sanderson muttered in a shocked voice. "How did she ever team up with Billy Farr?"

"I don't know. She must have run away from the convent, met him." Kate paused, then wheeled impulsively toward Frank. "Do you think he knew I was her mother?"

Sanderson had recovered from his surprise. "Doubt it. All he knew was that you had a lot of gold cached somewhere—and was going after it."

Kate dropped her eyes. "I can't seem to feel anything. I ought to cry. She was my own daughter—my own flesh and blood. It's hard to understand."

He took her in his arms. "No it's not. You've been apart a long time. She was a stranger to you."

From beyond the doorway a voice called, "There is someone in there? Speak!" It was Mendoza.

"Come in, Captain," Sanderson answered.

The officer, trailed by two men, walked into the room and halted. Mendoza was dust-covered and wore a bandage on his left arm. There was a blood smear on his neck. He squinted at Sanderson.

"It is you, *amigo!* Two of those we follow from the beginning. I expect to find you with the gold—not the young tigers in the yard. The others, what of them?"

"All dead."

Mendoza sighed. "It is sad. I too bring a brave man home to a widow, a wounded one to his wife."

Frank pointed to the pile of litter. "We never had the gold, Captain. You'll find the rest of it there."

The Rurale frowned as though not hearing. He said something in quick Spanish. One of the men picked up the fourth saddlebag and dug into its contents. Pablo Mendoza rubbed at his chin, smiling quizzically.

"All this is difficult to comprehend, *señor. I* thought—"

"Hard to explain. We went after the gold. Billy, out there, ended up with it. But you've got it now—all of it."

"You did not have to tell of this bag."

"We know that. Ought to square us with your government."

"Of a certainty. But why—"

"Don't ask me any questions I can't answer. If it's all right with you, the lady and I'll rest up here a bit and then head back across the border."

Mendoza considered that. He shrugged. "There is no objection."

Sanderson, one arm supporting Kate, moved toward the doorway. She held back momentarily, facing the Rurale.

"The girl—will she get a decent burial?"

"Of course, *señora*. Both will be placed in the churchyard. It is of importance to you?"

Kate nodded and stepped out into the hot sunshine with Sanderson. The bodies of Meg and Billy Farr were being carried away. They watched until the men had turned the corner of a house and were lost to view.

"I feel this was all my fault," Kate said in a faraway voice. "I failed her. If only I—"

"Too late for that kind of thinking," Frank broke in sternly. "You did what you had to do. Question is, what now?"

She turned to him. "I'll ask that of you."

He looked off across the baked flats. An old man, leading a string of burros loaded with firewood, was just coming over the rim of the valley.

"You told me once that I ought to go back to Kansas Bend—make a new start. I think I could

163

do that if you were with me."

"A new start," she repeated softly. "It would be that for both of us."

"Will you come?"

She smiled up at him. "I'll come, Frank," she said.